I0690230

PRINTHOUSEBOOKS PRESENTS:

ADORATION;

Love Unconditional.

Fiction

Book 1; Erotic Love Series.

An Erotic Love Series by ANTWAN 'ANT' BANK$

All PrintHouse Books titles also available at
PrintHouseBooks.com

PrintHouse Books, Atlanta, GA.

www.PrintHouseBooks.com

VIP INK Publishing Group, Inc.

Cover art by Sk7. *Published 9-6-2012*

Paperback isbn: 978-0-9886428-0-5

Library of Congress Cataloging-in-Publication Data.

ANTWAN 'ANT' BANK$

ADORATION; Love Unconditional/ ANTWAN 'ANT' BANK$

1. Erotica 2.Romance 3.Urban 4.Love 5.African American

6.ANTWAN 'ANT' BANK$

Printed in the United States of America

Dear Reader,

The word Adoration can be defined as fervent and devoted love or simply put; to worship. During our time on Earth we will all experience this powerful thing called Love. This novel will take you on a journey seen through the eyes of four couples and their relationships. For Love we endure amazing things and some of us will go to the limit to keep it.

Love can fill your heart with joy or leave it filled with hate. Adoration explores love at several levels; some of them good; some bad. In Book One of this Series; hearts will break, tears will fall, blood will shed and bells will chime; all in the name of love.

Dedicated to Tia, Tierra and Ashley.

ANTWAN 'ANT' BANK$

ADORATION

Love Unconditional

Book 1

VIP INK Publishing Group, Inc.

Atlanta, GA.

Table of Contents

1, N.Y.C.

The two fellas, Jeron and Tim grew restless waiting outside in the line to enter the club. It's the middle of January of 1993 in the Big Apple; Teddy Riley's new style of music; New Jack swing had just begun to take over the music scene.

Gentlemen wore suits, ties and dress shoes; Ladies, crazy hair styles, big ear rings and bright colors. Jeron and Tim brushed the snow off the shoulders of their black trench coats; stepped out of line and walked over to the VIP entrance.

Jeron a handsome brown skinned brother, stood 5'11'' with an average build; high top fade and goatee. Tim, a tall light skinned brother wore a mustache and low fade; people always said he looked like Al B Sure. The holidays had just passed and it was a new year, so to celebrate; the guys left their barracks out in West Point to come party in the city. The gentlemen approached the VIP entrance and had a few words with the doorman.

Hey fellas, do you guys have reservations for a table? Nah my man, we're tired of standing in that damn line that aint moving and getting snowed on. Ha-ha-ha. Is that right, well what do you want me to do about it?

Come on playboy, give us a break and let a few soldiers in my man. Dude I know you aint no soldier; looking like Mr. B. Sure. Man that wasn't funny; look we are officers over at West Point and came down to the city to meet some sexy ladies and have a good time. Alright, alright, show me your military I.D and I will let you guys in. My man, that's what I'm talking about! Jeron reached inside his coat pocket and pulled out his wallet and showed the doorman his I.D.

Tim reached in his back pocket to retrieve his and showed it to the doorman as well. Ok have a good time fellas and don't cause any damn trouble. The doorman stepped aside to let the guys pass. Thanks big man! Yeah, no problem guys!

They push the door open and go inside, cigarette smoke filled the air; New Jack City by Guy is playing over the speakers. "New... Jack Cityyyyy" "New.... Jack Cityyyyy".

Yo Tim, now this is what's happening! You can say that again J! Club Rain was a huge warehouse with two levels and a bar that sat in the center of the first floor. The second level was only six steps up from the first and wrapped around the entire club overlooking the first floor. Brass rails ran along the edge of the second level protecting the patrons from falling down onto the first where the dance floor was. White satin curtains back dropped the walls on the entire second level where all the VIP sections were located.

Plush royal blue sectionals and black marble center tables decorated all twelve VIP booths. At the entrance of the VIP level stood a short white male who was responsible for monitoring the V.I.P area. Come on Tim let's go down to the dance floor; that's where the girls are dawg. Hold on player, you don't wanna get a VIP booth?

Hell nah man; let's go down there with all the people; aint hardly nobody up here! Ok lead the way bruh! The fellas head toward the stairway where the bouncer was standing. Excuse me dawg, we need to get out. No problem sir, will you guys be coming back? Nah we're going to hang out on the first level with all the people. Ok sir, you guys have a good time! You do the same my man! Tim shook the gentleman's hand and walked down the stairs.

Damn it's a lot of bitches in this motherfucker! Hell yeah it is, I'm about to get me at least three numbers tonight Tim; bet that! Yeah I hear you Captain; we'll see how many you got when the night is over. Jeron makes his way through the crowded dance floor and over to the bar; Tim spots a group of ladies over at a table and heads in their direction. Yo J! Yo J! Jeron turns around. Yeah! Get me a Corona; I'm going over here with these ladies. Ok bruh, got you! Jeron approaches the bar.

Hello sir, what can I get for you? Let me get one Corona and a Long Island Ice Tea. Will there be anything else sir? Nope that's it for now baby! Ok! The Dj turns down the music and makes an announcement. What's up all my beautiful people; I like to give a birthday shout out to my home girl Simone! Here's your request baby; go get your dance on! Happy Birthday baby; let's wind up with Shabba Ranks and Telephone Love! The patrons start to cheer and crowd the dance floor; the music went up a few notches higher and the disco lights went from red to green to blue.

"Telephone Love, you sound so sweet on the line" "Telephone love, you make my day every time". Tim finally approaches the ladies. Hello ladies, you guys are all looking lovely tonight. Thank you, you don't look bad yourself Mr.! Thanks, I'm Tim by the way; what's you guys names? Oh, I'm Tonya! Hi, I'm Lisa! Hi, I'm Simone and it's my birthday! Well nice to meet you ladies and happy birthday Simone! Thank you! So why are you here all by yourself Tim?

Oh, I'm not alone; I'm with my best friend Jeron; he's over at the bar right now. Ok because I was starting to wonder! Wonder about what Tonya! Why a sexy man like you was here alone! Ha-ha-ha. We just came down from West Point to hang out.

Simone stood up and started dancing. Hold on, this is my favorite part! "When you call I feel so good" "Wish you were living in my neighborhood" "So you can hang up the phone and rush on over" "Take up where we left, telephone in the cover". You go girl! Wind that booty! Ha-ha-ha. Shut up Lisa! So where's your friend Tim?

He's walking over this way now! Where is he? He's that guy right there; with the high top fade and goatee holding two drinks. Oh

I see him! Look Simone; he's handsome girl and your type too bitch! Simone continued to dance but slowed down just a little to see what Jeron looked like. Tonya; look girl! Look at what Bitch! Your damn sister, she's checking that man out girl!

Good, her ass needs a man, so she can get out of momma's house! Ha-ha-ha. Bitch, you is stupid! Simone stopped dancing then picked up her glass of wine from the table; she put the glass to her sexy soft lips and took a sip.

The red lipstick she wore complemented her butter pecan skin tone; her silky black hair was layered and cut in the latest Halle Berry style. Her diamond cut necklace and 14kt ear rings blinged under the club lights and the black dress she wore fell right above her knee high boots.

J makes his way over to Tim and the ladies. Here you go bruh, one Corona! Thanks J! Ladies this is my best friend Jeron! Hi Jeron!

J this is Tonya, that young lady is Lisa and that's...

Um... hmmmm... Excuse me! I can introduce myself! How are you Jeron, I'm Simone; nice to meet you. Hello Simone nice to meet you too; you wouldn't happen to be the Simone the Dj gave a birthday shout out to! Yes that is me; the one and only baby! Well happy birthday gorgeous; can I buy you a drink? Yes! I thought you would never ask! Ha-ha-ha. I'm a gentleman always baby; I like that dress on you too. Ummmm. You're just full of compliments, aren't you?

Hey just letting you know how I feel baby! I can appreciate that Jeron; I love an honest man. Well damn; this bitch done forgot about me and you over here! Let a bitch meet some new dick and she lose her mind; look at her Tonya. Child I see it; don't hate on my sister. Ha-ha-ha.

Shut up girl; your crazy ass. Simone! Simone! What girl! We're going to the bar;

you want another drink? Yeah, can I get another Merlot! Sure sis; I got it! Hey Tim; are you coming with us? Sure let's go! Simone and Jeron are sitting down at the table.

Tim and the other ladies walk across the crowded dance floor and head toward the bar. Well! Well what Simone! Tell me something about yourself; are you from New York? Oh no! Not me, I'm a country boy. Ha-ha-ha. Oh really! How country is country?

You talking; backwoods Alabama! Ha-ha-ha. I'm saying let a girl know! You a trip, no I'm from S.C! S.C; what's that! South Carolina! Ok, you're a Carolina boy. So why are you in the Big Apple? Tim and I are both officers in the Army at West Point. No shit! Officer huh! Yep! Officers! How about you Simone; are you from New York? Yes sir; Long Island. L.I is cool; my aunt stays up there; not far from Prospect Ave. Wow really; stop playing! No I'm dead serious; my sisters and I use to go there every summer.

Yeah I hear you; you don't know anything about L.I. What part did she live in then? Ha-ha-ha. Really; you wanna test me right now. Well answer me officer! She lives in Westbury! Ok, ok, maybe you know a little something. Ha-ha-ha. Whatever Simone! So now that you know where I live; you can come visit me when you come to visit your aunt or vice versa. Oh so I take it that's a date then. Yeah; you can say that! I don't want to step on any ones toes; are you single? Well that's a long story! I got time; tell me about it.

Fuck it! I'm married! There I said it! Well damn; your husband must be pretty bad to make you wanna cheat on him. He's a piece of shit, is what he is; fucker cheated on me and left me with two daughters; now I'm back home staying with my parents. Damn, I'm sorry to hear that baby. You don't have to apologize; it's not your fault man. His ass was military too; damn sorry ass aint even seen his baby girl yet. Wow, really!

Yep! That fool left me when I was 6 months pregnant; now I have to start all over with two kids; what man is going to want me now? Well; love isn't prejudice; the heart wants what the heart wants. Hmm-Hmm. I hear you; I bet you don't want to talk to me now; do you? Well actually; I'm more attractive to you now. Why is that? Because you were honest and told me the truth; you could have lied. Does that mean you like me? Yeah I think you're a cool person so far; I mean you can always get crazy later! Ha-ha-ha. Stop it!

Jeron stands up and grabs her by the hand then leads her on to the dance floor. Wait a minute officer; who said I wanted to slow dance with you? Come on baby; this is my song! J starts to sing along with the music. Who is this singing Jeron? It's Mint Condition; Pretty Brown Eyes. They walk to the center of the floor; embraced each other and sway slowly from side to side. "Pretty brown eyes, you know I see you""It's a disguise, the way you treat me"

"You keep holding on, to your thought of rejection, if you're with me you're secured".

Tonya, Tim and Lisa had made their way back over to the table. Damn, where's my sister; that fool left her purse on the chair. Girl she can't be far if she left her purse; I'm sure she's close. Tim stops by the table and with his 6'4" statue; he scans the club. Oh there she is; right there with J on the dance floor.

They all look over to the dance floor and spot Simone and Jeron hugged up with each other. Tonya your sister looks like she's in love girl. Lisa; leave her alone, let her enjoy the moment. Girl I'm just saying; I bet oh boy get that ass tonight. So what if she gives it up; that's her business! Hey Tim! Yes Ma'am! Which one of us you like; me or Lisa? Ha-ha-ha. Both you guys are cool. Yeah we know that but you aint fucking both of us Mr.! Tonya you need to stop tripping; I have a man! Bitch that aint your man; that nigga is a puppet!

Tonya kiss my black ass; hey it was nice meeting you Tim; I am about to go home and get me some. Bye Tonya; call me tomorrow bitch. Smack! Ouch! Tonya slaps Lisa on the ass as he walks off. Girl bye and that shit hurts; why you do it so hard! Stop crying; I'll call you; good night! Bye! Lisa leaves the club and heads home.

You guys must have known each other a long time? Yeah, we all grew up together; Lisa was our next door neighbor from kindergarten to high school. Yeah, you guys seem really close. Enough about that; let's go get a VIP booth and a bottle of champagne. I'm down; let's do it!

Hold on let me take Simone her purse; I'll be right back. Tonya took the purse and walked over to J and her sister on the dance floor. Here you are sis; we are going over to get a VIP booth; you guys come up when you're done making out. Ha-ha-ha. What the fuck ever sis! We'll see you guys in a bit! Ok sis!

Tonya grabbed Tim by the hand and lead him through the crowded dance floor and over to the VIP where the short bouncer was waiting by the stairway. I see you came back brother; I don't think we have any free booths now though. Hold on a minute let me go check. The gentleman walked up the stair way and looked over the VIP to see if any booths were available. He turns around and walks back over to Tim and Tonya. Hey my man; you're in luck we have one on the far end. That's what's up! Thanks my man! No problem brother; will your partner be coming back over too. Who Jeron? Yeah, if that's the guy you came in with.

Yeah, he will be coming in a few with a young lady. Ok my man; I will show them where you are. My man; good looking out dawg! Hey it's what I get paid for brother; don't mention it. He and Tim shake hands before they part ways.

Damn baby; did you know that guy? No, why you say that? He was acting super nice and he didn't even charge us for the booth.

Ha-ha-ha. We came in the club through the VIP entrance so we met him when we first got in; that's how he knew me. Oh ok; now that makes sense. I got a question for you Tim. What is it Tonya? I want to fuck you so bad right now; it's been like 6 months since I had sex. Damn; why so long? You know; I don't know why; I've just been stuck home with my kids trying to be a single mom and never took anytime for myself. Time just flew by; now I'm horny as fuck and asking you for some dick.

Ha-ha-ha. Wow! I can't believe I just said that but I am serious as fuck. So you're asking me for some and you just met me? Yep! So are you gonna give me some or not? Ha-ha-ha. Where? In the VIP booth man! You serious; aren't you? Well not about the VIP booth but we can get a room or something; we can't go to my place; the baby sitter is there with my rug rats. How many kids do you have Tonya?

I have two boys and two girls, the boys are 5 year old twins and my girls are 2 and 3.

Wow, where's their father? Man that fool is on Riker's Island for the next 10 years on a dope charge. I aint had no sex since he left 5 months ago!

Well, if you really want to do this; we can. Hell yes, you promise! Yes; we can get a room after we leave here. Thank you handsome; please don't think bad of me. I'm just tired of being lonely; I need a man in my life. Hey, you don't have to explain; I understand.

The couple made their way over to the booth and takes a seat on the couch. Tonya leaned over to kiss Tim on the cheek. Muah! What was that for? For being a gentleman and not thinking bad of me! Hey enough of that already, it will be our secret; ok!

Oh look; here comes my sister and your boy. Jeron and Simone enter the VIP booth. Man this chic will dance all night long; I had to pull her ass off the floor dawg. Ha-ha-ha.

Shut up J; you weren't complaining when I was backing this ass up on you.

Ha-ha-ha. Because you sexy mommy! Yeah, tell me something I don't already know! What yall got going on over here bruh? We just chilling man; getting to know each other. Jeron reaches in his pocket and pulls out a pack of gum.

Here you go Simone; have one. Thanks! Oh hell nah; wait a minute! Are you trying to say something J! What? Just take the gum baby; it's really good. Ha-ha-ha. What the fuck are you laughing at Tim? Nothing Simone; you crazy; you two make a great couple. Jeron opens a piece of gum and sticks it in Simone's mouth.

Ha-ha-ha. Damn sis; eat that shit! Ha-ha-ha. Keep it up J; I'm gonna bust you up! Yeah, yeah I hear yah. Yo Tim, I'm about to leave bruh; I got drill in the morning. Simone; call me when you get up tomorrow. Are you sure about that; my little girl gets up really early! Baby I'm sure; I will be up first. He leans over and kisses her on the lips. Tim, later bruh! Alright dawg; I'm gone chill for a bit; see you on the base. Jeron leaves the club and heads back to West Point.

Hey Tonya, are you ready to leave and where the fuck is Lisa? Not yet sis; I'm going to catch a ride with Tim; Lisa was flirting with some dude over by the bar on her way out. Well; you be safe and Tim it was nice meeting you; I am taking my butt home. Bye sis! Bye! Tonya took both of her legs off the floor and placed them across Tim's lap. The bottom of her dress rolled up to her thigh. Tim removed her heels and begun to massage her feet.

Hmmmm. That feels so good; I'm getting wet just from you touching me. Stop lying girl! I'm serious man; it's been a long time since I've had a man's touch. Keith Sweat's; Make it last forever is playing in the background. "Make it last forever, forever" "Don't let our love end" "Don't let our love end".

Tonya opened her legs; rolled upward and straddled Tim. Their lips begin to touch; right before she stuck her tongue in his mouth. Both their hormones were sizzling; some hot sexy shit was about to go down; him being hard as a rock and her being backed up for the last six months.

The fuse was lit and the dynamite was about to explode. She unzipped Tim's pants; slid back to look down at it; reached down and slid her panties to the side then slid his Johnson right in her, fat, throbbing, juicy vagina.

Her loud moans fell silent under the loud club speakers; tear drops fell from her eyes, filled with both joy and relief. She rode him like a horse; back and forth, up slow, down slow, up slow, down slow she went.

Yes! This feels so good baby; I don't ever want to stop. You like that; huh, you like that. Yeah I like it baby, I like it. Tim slid his hands away from her hips and back around to her ass cheeks. As she rode him; he pulled her ass cheeks apart to open her pussy wider.

Yessss, Yesssss, Yesssss, that feels so good right now, damn you fucking the shit out of me right now. Whose dick is this baby? I said whose dick is this baby? Ohhhhhh, this is my dick baby! This is my dick! Damn, you're wetter than Niagara Falls baby; I like that shit.

Ummmm-mmmmm. This pussy juicy! I'm gone call your butt wet-wet. Call me whatever you want baby, as long as I can ride this cock of yours. Well stop talking bitch and ride it then, don't stop wet-wet, give it to me baby. Oh yes baby, yes I'm about to come! She screamed under the loud music. Come on baby, get your nut; I know you ready to bust baby; come on. He whispered in her ear as she continued to ride.

Oh God! Oh God! Oh God! Yesssss! Whooooo! Hooooo! Damn Tonya, you came all over my pants; that damn wet-wet aint no joke! Ha-ha-ha. You silly! Tonya grabbed her red heels off the couch; got up off of him and sat on the chair. She opened her legs then slid her panties back over; put on her heels then stood up to pull down her red dress. That was terrific; we must do it again soon baby.

Oh yeah, you liked that sexy? Yes I did baby! Come on; let's go get a few shots before we head home. Sure but let me get my coat from coat check first; I will meet you by the bar. Ok; I'll go order the drinks! Tim and Tonya exited VIP and head down the stairway; she went left; he went towards the bar. Excuse me! Excuse me! Bartender! Yes sir; what can I get you? Let me get two double shots of tequila! Coming right up!

The bartender put two glasses on the bar and poured two double shots of Jose'. The crowd started cheering as the Dj played the next track. EPMD's; You gots to chill. "Relax your mind, let your conscience be free and get down to the sounds of EPMD" "Well you should be quiet while the MC rap but if you tired - - then go take a nap".

A few minutes had passed and Tonya had not made her way over to the bar yet. Tim stands there looking around the club to see if he could spot her but there was no sign of Tonya in sight. Growing impatient he picked up his shot and took it to the head; waited about a minute then took hers too.

He reached in his pocket and peeled a $20 bill off his bank roll and left it on the bar. He walked around the club looking for her but still no sign then he approached the coat check. Excuse me Ms.! Yes sir! Did you see a dark skinned young lady in a red dress with shoulder length hair and red pumps?

Oh; you're talking about Tonya? Yes that's her! Yeah she left a few minutes ago; her husband sent a limo to pick her up! Her husband! Yes Sir; he owns the place! Well I'll be damn; aint that a bitch! Excuse me sir! Nothing baby; thanks; you have a good night!

Tim gathered himself and walked out the club; still in shock from what just happened.

He walked a few blocks down to where his truck was parked; all the while thinking to himself. Man I can't believe that bitch just hustled me for my dick.

Ha-ha-ha. Wait until J here's about this shit. The streets of Manhattan were jammed as always on a Friday night. Tim made his way into the parking deck to get his vehicle then pulled out into the busy traffic and headed back to base.

2, West Point.

Its 5:00 AM the next morning; the guys are all outside in formation preparing for their daily 4 mile run. Jeron spots Tim dragging ass in the back of formation while the other soldiers are stretching; he walks over to him. Bruh what the fuck happened to your ass last night; you got drunk didn't you fool?

Dude you're not going to believe this shit. Believe what! I fucked Tonya in the VIP booth last night; when we got done I went over to the bar to get us a few shots and she went over to get her jacket from coat check. I'm standing there at the bar with the drinks; waiting for her to come over so we could take the shots, you know. Ok; what happened?

Man this girl aint even come back to the bar, so I started looking for her; no sign of the bitch. I drunk both the shots then walked over to coat check to see if she indeed checked a coat. Well did she? Dude the lady in coat check knew her and said she gave her the coat a few minutes ago but Tonya left soon after because her husband sent a Limo to pick her up; turns out this nigga owns the club.

Ha-ha-ha. Now that's some crazy shit bruh! Ha-ha-ha. Only in New York City! Was it good though bruh? Man she got that wet-wet; you got to ask her sister what the fucking deal is? Bruh don't tell me your feelings hurt over that; hell; we do it all the time!

Man just be sure and find out the deal when you talk to Simone! Ok my man; I got you; let's go get these 4 miles in though. The Soldiers jump in formation with the other officers. The drill instructor calls the company to attention. Company! Attention!

Mark time! March! Double time; March! The soldiers left running up the hill on their way to the first mile of four.

Ring-Ring-Ring-Ring. Hello! Get your butt up sis! I'm up Simone; what the hell do you want girl; can a bitch get some sleep! So what happened girl? Did you go back to his place?

Hell no; I fucked that fool in VIP. Ooooooh; you nasty bitch; was it good! What! That nigga had me creaming all over the damn place. Did anybody see yall; you know Craig be having spies all over the club. I have no idea and don't care; that fool sent a Limo to pick me up before I could tell Tim bye!

So I know he's pissed and he's for sure gonna have Jeron ask you about me. Damn; what you want me to do? Give him my number; Craig's whore ass doesn't answer the phone no way. Ok girl I'll do that; I will talk to you later; I got to fix the kids some breakfast. Alright, later sis!

Tonya! What Craig! Where's my blue tie? Look in the top drawer! Thanks; I got it! Are you going to cook breakfast today; what a man got to do to get his wife to make him some damn eggs around here? Craig, don't start that crap early this morning; I'm not in the mood for your shit. Then fix me some breakfast and I will shut up.

Damn, I'm gone make you some eggs man; stop crying already. Thank you Wife! So did you have fun at the club last night? It was cool; Simone enjoyed her-self.

Good; tell sis I said happy birthday but did you enjoy yourself? Yes I had a good time as well. That's good baby; you need to be careful with that flirting too; don't have me fuck nobody up! What are you talking about Craig? Don't play stupid Tonya! How did you want your eggs baby?

Ha-ha-ha. You just gone change the subject; just like that huh! Do you want them scrambled with cheese or can I make you an omelet. Fuck it! Don't worry about it; I will get something on the way to my meeting. Craig; wait! Go to hell Tonya!

Let me find out that you're giving my pussy away; I'm going to beat your ass then find that nigga and kill him right in front of you! Baby you tripping! Craig snatches his coat off the chair and storms out the front door. BAM! He slammed the door behind him.

Karen, Kristy, Donny, Darrel come down stairs and eat some breakfast! Ok mommy! Tonya fries up half a dozen of eggs, some bacon and made a pot of grits. The kids came running downstairs into the kitchen.

Donny, get the glasses; Darrel get the juice out of the fridge and make the drinks. Girls sit down; come on guys hurry; you got school and daycare. Mommy has to work today! Mommy! Mommy! Can I have some chocolate milk? Please Mommy!

No Kristy; there's not enough for everyone; drink your orange juice baby. Ok mommy. She brings the plate of eggs over to the table and begins to fix the kids plates. Here you go guys; grits; eggs and bacon; eat up!

Tonya walked over to the kitchen counter and picked up the phone to make a call. Ring-Ring-Ring. Hello; thanks for calling

West Coast Image! Hi Tina; this is Tonya! Hey Tonya; what's up boss? Can you let my assistant Sonya know I will be about 10 minutes late! No problem honey; I will let her know. Thanks baby! Click! She hangs up.

Back on base the guys are getting ready for a long work day; Jeron was just stepping out of the shower when the phone rings. Ring-Ring-Ring. Hello! Hey you! Hey; who's speaking? You get one guess officer. Ha-ha-ha. Hello Simone; how are you baby?

I'm good; what are you doing? Well, I just got out of the shower, now I'm about to get dressed for work. I'm sorry; do you want me to call you back? No hold on; I will put you on speaker phone. Ok baby! Did you enjoy your birthday last night?

Hell yeah; I had a ball. That's good; how old are you by the way? I'm 24 now! Really! Yes; why you say that? I'm 24 too! Ha-ha-ha. Ok! I spoke to Tim this morning; he told me what happened. What did he tell you? He said your sister left him at the club without saying good bye. Her ass was probably drunk; she spaces out when she drinks too much. He also said that someone told him she was married.

Yep; that she is! Damn; why didn't she tell my man that shit; your sis got some issues I see. Don't say it like that baby; she means well. Really; what did her husband have to say about that? Those two fools are always fighting; shit I don't think they are even sleeping in the same room. That marriage is over; they're just sticking it out for the kids! That's too bad; tell her to call my man and let him know what's up; he is pissed about that situation.

I will let her know today; as soon as I speak with her. Thanks; I appreciate that Simone. Your welcome! So when am I going to see you again? When did you want to see me baby? How about tonight? You don't waist anytime, do you girl! Nope! I get off at 5pm today; you can come over if you want. Thanks for the invite! Your welcome! So are you coming over?

Yes; I'm thinking around 7pm. Cool; I will talk to you later then I'm about to go get some chow. Alright baby, have a good day at work. Thanks; later! Knock-Knock. Who is it! It's Tim Cap! Hold on Lieutenant! He walks over to unlock the door. What's up bruh; everything good? I'm good man; let's go eat dawg.

Hold on; let me get my hat. Jeron grabs his hat off the dresser and heads down to the mess hall with Tim. The two officers walked down the long tan stonewall hallway on the white tiled buffed floors. Bruh I was on the phone with Simone for like 30 minutes; she's coming over tonight after work. My man; you moving fast; aint you dude? Hey, it's all good; I don't think she's a psycho.

I hope not bruh; you don't need that drama on base. I aint worried about that man; I asked her about her sister too. What did she have to say? She said that she's married but she and her husband don't even sleep in the same bed anymore; they're only sticking it out for the kids.

Damn; she could have told me that! Bruh don't even trip; you got the pussy didn't you! Yeah but that was some dirty shit! That bitch walked away without saying anything.

Calm down dude; you acting like a girl right now; she's gonna call you later. Whatever Cap! Tim and J enter the mess hall and take their place in line. So how's that Blackburn investigation going? That case is almost closed; Blackburn is set to get off active duty next Friday but we're picking his ass up and shipping him to Leavenworth.

Damn; he's going to be a mad motherfucker; how did you guys catch him? We sent in a female undercover MP; she rode with him on a few transactions. Man you cats are dirty; was she fine? Hell yeah; she was! Ha-ha-ha. What was he pushing? A few pounds of marijuana; he was selling it to a few soldiers as well as civilians. Damn; are yall arresting the soldiers too?

No; we're kicking them out and giving them dishonorable discharges. The two officers approached the chow line. Good morning officers; what are you guys having today? Let me get some pancakes and sausage baby! I'll have the same sweet heart! Ok, coming right up!

Once you finish that case J; I'm gone need help with some of the new cadet interviews. No problem; I got you bruh! The officers take a seat at the lunch table alongside 4 other soldiers. What's up soldiers! Yo what up Cap! LT! Chow time baby; that's all. What's new at the point fellas? Shit; we're shipping out to Saudi in 72 hours Cap.

Damn; good luck with that! Thanks cap! What you got plan tonight Tim? Man I'm going to the pool hall to hustle a few cats. Ha-ha-ha. Alright, don't lose your check fool! Man I'm good; aint nobody taking my loot! Yeah I hear you; I'm charging 20% on all loans nigga! You funny Cap!

He then leans over to Jeron and speaks softly. So, are you going to keep all of the stash when you make the bust next week? I don't know; it depends on if we have a buyer by then. I know someone that might want it; I will call him after work. He lives in Brooklyn though!

I don't care if they live in Syracuse as long as the money is good. We got four months left in the military; I'm trying to have my bank account full of cash when I get out bruh! How about you?

Man you already know; I'm down for whatever! Then there is no more to be said; call him up. Alright Tim; I will get up with you later. Jeron got up from the table and exited the mess hall.

A female soldier sat down at the table beside Tim. Hey Sherry! How is everything over at B Company? It's good LT; how are things in Alpha? Things are outstanding! Well, I'm happy to hear that; how's Dana the new Captain doing; you guys still fooling around? Ha-ha-ha. She's fine and no we're not fooling around anymore. Why not? Man; that girl started tripping after she made C.O.

Hey; I'm sure she has her reasons. Yeah whatever; enough about her; she's old news. Ha-ha-ha. Is that right? Yep! What's up with you? Are you free later? That depends; what are you trying to do? Just go get a few drinks and maybe a bite. I will let you know; the day is just starting; maybe I will be available. Yeah, make sure you do that.

I'm late for work; call my office later and let me know. Alright; I will do that LT; have a good day. Jeron and Tim finished their food then headed to work.

Meanwhile, over on Long Island, Tonya had her hands full. Hey! Hey! Twins; calm your butts down back there and put on those seat belts! Mommy! Mommy! What is it Kristy? I want my blanky!

Baby girl; you have another one at the sitters! Tonya tries to drive and keep an eye on the kids at the same time as she heads to the school. Alright Donny and Darrel get your lunches; we're here. She stops the SUV by the curb where the principle is waiting to assist the students in the drop zone. Donny opens the door and gets out; Darrel follows. They both turn around and wave to their mother. Bye Mommy! Bye baby; see you guys later; be good; ok! Yes Ma'am! The principle escorts them in the building and Tonya pulls off and head to the sitter; two blocks up the way.

Beep! Beep! Tonya blows the horn when she pulls in front of the sitter's house. Gloria opened the door and waved them in. Tonya parked the truck and picked up her youngest and held the other by her hand as they walked inside.

Hello my little darlings; Auntie Gloria missed you! Muah! The sitter kissed the girls on the cheek. Ok Ms. Gloria; I will see you later; bye girls; be good now. Bye

Mommy! Tonya ran outside; jumped in the truck and raced to work; trying not to be too late.

She turns up the radio to listen to her cd; Real Love by Mary J Blige. "We are lovers through and through" "We made it through the storm" "I really want you to realize" "I really want to put you on".

Tonya begins to sing along as she's headed to work. I'm looking for a real love! Real love! I'm searching for a real love; baby! Yeah; real love!

Meanwhile back on Long Island; Simone had just left the house to walk up the block to Nathan's for a hot dog. Beep! Beep! A black explorer slowed up and tried to get her attention while she was walking.

Hey Simone! Hey Eddie! Where you headed? Nathans! You want a ride? No, I need to walk a little bit anyway. Alright see you later, tell your sister I said to call me. Bye Eddie! After a few more feet and 5 minutes later she arrived at her destination.

Simone entered Nathan's; only to find herself standing in a long line behind several customers. Pow! Pow! What the fuck was that? She ran over to the door to see what the noise was; no one else seemed to care. Just across the street was an old red pickup truck and an old man was standing there under the hood with his tools. The truck was making loud gun-shot like noises as the old gentlemen tried to get her started.

Order number 38! Order number 38 please! Simone turns around and jumps back in line to place her order. Hello Ma'am; what can I get for you today? Hi; can I have a number 2 please! Did you want a drink with that Ma'am? Yes, make that a Coke please! So, I have a number 2 with a coke? Yes!

Ok; here's your number and your total is $4.29. She hands the cashier a $5 dollar bill. Thank you; your order will be ready in a few minutes. The restaurant door opens; two male customers walk in. Damn nigga; I'm hungry as a motherfucker! Me too nigga!

The two guys were loud and disruptive; both wore black adidas sweat suits, white shell toe adidas and long dread locks. One of the guys walked to the front of the line. Excuse me; can I get a number one and a sprite! No sir; you need to get in line; you jumped all these people.

Oh shit! My bad! He reached in his pocket and pulled out a fat bank roll; peeled off a $20 bill and handed it to the first person in line. Here you go Miss; sorry about that! The patron smiled and took the money. Thank you and that's ok! Now can I order my food please! That was a number 1 and a sprite? Yep; ring it up.

That will be $3.79 sir! He reaches in his pocket and hands her a $10 bill. Here; make it two orders of the same thing! Ok sir! Keep the change! Thank you; here's your number sir. He took the number and headed over to the lobby with his friend.

Number 43! Number 43 please! Simone looks at her number and walks over to the counter to get her food. That's me! Here you go Ma'am; may I have your number please? Thank you; have a good day and come back to see us.

She heads towards the exit. Yo! Yo! Yeah you! What's up Mommy? Nothing; going home! Why are you leaving; sit down and chill with us. What's your name cutie? I'm Simone! Nice to meet you; I'm Tiger and that's my cousin Bobby. Nice to meet you fellas; that was so rude what you did earlier; jumping those people. Hey I wasn't thinking; I just wanted to eat! Ha-ha-ha. I did pay her though.

Yeah whatever! So why are you up here by yourself; where's your man? He's at home with the kids; waiting on me. Damn; he's a lucky motherfucker because you fine as hell. Thank you! Well, it was nice meeting you fellas; I have to go. Alright mommy, be easy.

Uptown; Tonya had just reached the City where she ran her Manhattan Model

Agency. She walked inside; hung her coat, picked up her mail from the receptionist and entered her office. Hey Boss! Hey Sonya; what's our schedule like today?

Busy as always! Ok, what do we have first? Let's see; we need 5 models for fight night at MSG this coming Saturday! What else we got? There's a video shoot in Harlem tomorrow at 6 Am; we need 10 girls for that and only 2 of them will get paid lead. Alright; have Tina get on the phones and schedule the models for a casting today. Yes Ma'am! I'm on it! Thanks Sonya! Tonya sat down at her glass top desk that sat in the center of her corner office.

Two white leather arm chairs sat in front of her desk; Tonya sat comfortably in her King sized white leather chair. The view of Time Square created a scenic backdrop framed by the large window that sat behind her chair and showed a bird's eye view from the 48th floor.

Ring-Ring-Ring. Hello! Tonya; I have the music video producer El Ray on the phone. Cool; put him through! She puts her phone on speaker. EL! What's happening man? Hey Tonya; how are you doing doll? I am doing great Baby! What can I help you with?

I need to add 3 male models for the video shoot tomorrow! That's not a problem; we will make sure everything is straight. Thanks doll; I will see you all at 6:00 am tomorrow. Shit! Who? You Tonya; you're coming aren't you? Yeah but not at 6 baby; I got kids to take care of before I can come to your set. Well, I guess you can be late.

Whatever EL! Bye Man! Later doll! Click! They hang up then Tonya calls Simone. Ring-Ring-Ring Hello! Hey sis! Hey Tonya, what's up? I was sitting here thinking about last night and I feel bad for leaving Tim like that; can you get his number from Jeron; I want to apologize. Yeah sure; that was fucked up though. Shut up Simone; I said I am going to apologize. What are you doing right now; it sounds pretty quiet at your house. Girl I just left Nathan's; I got me a number two and a coke. I am about to dig in as soon as you hang up! Ha-ha-ha. Bye sis, go eat! Bye; I will get that number for you when I go on base tonight too. Thanks slut!

What! I know your butt aint talking! Ha-ha-ha. Click! I know this bitch didn't just hang up on me! Tonya stood up from her desk and headed towards the receptionist area. Tina! Yes Ma'am? How are we coming on the casting calls? I am half way through the call backs now. Ok, stay on pace; we have a lot of work to do. Yes Ma'am.

Oh Tina; one more thing! Get the photographer up here to set up for the casting; he should be upstairs in the studio. Yes Ma'am.

Ring-Ring-Ring. Hello, West Coast Image how may I help you? Hey Sonya; this is Simone; can I speak to Tonya please? Sure Simone; hold on. Tonya! Yes Ma'am! Your sister is on line one. Ok, I'll get it in my office. She walks over to her desk to pick up the phone. Hey sis; what's up? Sis; I need a favor! Yeah what is it?

Please, please could you pick up the kids for me while I go to West Point? I meant to ask you earlier. I guess so girl; gone and get that ass waxed; hell it's been about six months right! Ha-ha-ha. Kiss my ass sis! Ha-ha-ha. Well it's true! No it's only been four months!

Shit that's long enough; go have some fun; I got you covered. Alright thank you baby; I love you! Bye! Hold on Bitch; what time are you coming to get your rug rats? Ha-ha-ha. Around 11 tonight! Ok see you then and don't forget to give Tim my number. Thanks and I got you sis! Alright later!

Ring-Ring-Ring. Hello! Hey Jeron! Hey who's this? This is Simone! Hello gorgeous; how are you? I'm great baby; how are you? Just getting home from work; are you coming over? Yep I am getting dressed now;

what building are you in? I'm in building 578, room 270; what time are you coming? I'm leaving in 20 minutes; should be there within the hour. Cool; I'm going to wash up and put on some clothes; see you in a few. Great! I can't wait to see you baby! I can't wait to see you either gorgeous. Bye! Click!

They hang up the phone and J goes in the bathroom to start the shower. His room was in the officer's quarters equipped with a small kitchen, dull grey floors, military issued bed, table and wall chest. Two black love seats sat against the white stone wall under the only window, across the room sitting in the corner was a maple wood finished entertainment center.

One 40 inch Samsung TV and 5 disc changer pioneer stereo system sat in the center of the entertainment stand. Cologne scented incents sat in small Buddha holders on top of the end tables and entertainment center. J came out of the bathroom; turned on the red light and cassette player; R-Kelly's; Slow Dance was the song of choice. "Slow dance

(Slow dance)" "I just wanna slow dance with you" "Slow dance (Slow)" "Oh, oh, oh, oh".

Jeron removed all of his clothes and placed them in the basket in the corner of his room; then entered the bathroom to get in the shower. Knock-Knock. Damn; who is it! He yelled from the shower. Hey it's Gracie; can I borrow your Mary J cd? Yeah come in; it's on the table Gracie; lock that door behind you too please. Thanks Cap! No problem LT!

Gracie was a second Lieutenant who just got transferred from Germany to West Pointe; her and J went out a few times but never got to first base. Jeron was old fashioned and didn't believe in forcing himself on a lady; if she was feeling him then it would come naturally.

Gracie on the other hand was really attractive to him but her up-bringing as an Asian woman didn't allow her to be too aggressive. She was a beautiful woman;

5'4" in statue, cream colored skin, shoulder length black hair and a gorgeous smile.

Hey Cap; I will bring it back in a few, ok; I just want to make a copy. Alright no problem; just keep it until tomorrow; I have company coming over. Gracie picked up the cd from the table; paused for a minute; looked around then left the room without saying a word; leaving the door unlocked still.

Cap thought he heard her leave and started calling out for her. Gracie! Gracie! Gracie! There was no answer. He turned off the shower; dried off and went up front to put on his clothes; a grey Army T-shirt and black shorts along with his Nike sandals.

Ring-Ring-Ring. His phone rings; he looks down at it and contemplates if he should answer it or let the answering machine pick it up. Simone was on the way over and he didn't want to chance answering the phone; it could have been one of his other lady friends. 10 seconds had passed and the answering machine picked up the call.

"Hello, thank you for calling, this is Captain Briggs; sorry I missed your call but if you would leave your name, number and reason for calling; I will return your call as soon as possible." Hi J, this is Erin; I really had a great time the other night and wanted to see you later; call me back when you get this message; bye baby. Jeron went to the mirror and started picking his hair; a smirk came across his face as he listened to her message.

He starts to sing along with the music. "I wanna pull her close to me (pull her close to me)" "And whisper sweet things in her ear, oh yeah" "Cause tonight I'm full of fire baby, oh yeah". You're the only one I wanna slow dance with, Simone, Simone... Come on Simone.....

Knock-Knock. Who is it! It's Simone baby! He runs to open the door. Hey, come in baby; let me get your coat; make yourself comfortable. Thank you baby; oh snap; you got the red light on huh. Yep! Shit girl; you're looking sexy as hell in those jeans though! Thank you; you like! Simone turns around and models for him.

It smells good in here baby; what kind of incents are those? They're called midnight love and I also have one called romance too. Look at you Mr. Lover man; got the slow jams on too; you think you're getting some pussy huh? Ha-ha-ha. That's up to you gorgeous but yes I do. Ha-ha-ha. Come here lover man.

Simone grabs Cap by the rim of his shorts and pulls him close to her; their noses touch as they looked in each other's eyes. Her soft lips touched his then both their mouths opened slightly and his tongue begin to dance with hers. Simone nipples became erect as J massaged her butt cheeks and rubbed his hard penis against her vagina.

Jeron slid his hands from her ass and up under her shirt where he unsnapped the back of her bra which fell to the floor. Simone then lifted up her arms so he could remove her top. As the top came off; J went in closer and started sucking on her nipples.

Simone released sounds of passion and joy; a feeling she haven't experienced in a while. Ooohhh that feels so good baby; don't stop. You like that gorgeous; let me do the other one. Oooohhhh that feels good! Give me that dick baby; give it to me now. She reached down and pulled the draw string on his shorts; they fell to the floor and his penis stood there erect; all nine inches. Yeah Simone; Its right there baby! Show me what you're going to do with it!

Oooohhhh gosh; it looks good baby. J stroked his dick in a slow motion while waiting for her to make the next move. She dropped to her knees and removed Caps hands and replaced it with her own. Simone stroked the Captain's penis with her right then raised it up a little so she could lick his balls. Hmmmmm; yeah baby; that's it; lick them nuts. You like that baby; does it feel good to yuh? Hell yeah I do!

Jeron reaches down and grabs the lady by her hair; pulled her mouth away from his nuts. Open up baby; let me slide my hard cock down your throat. Simone opens wide; Cap softly slaps her lips with the head of his penis; she sticks out her tongue as if to say; put it in.

Jeron obliges her and inserts it in her pie whole; he could feel the ridges on her gums as his penis hit the roof of her mouth and the head hit the back of her throat.

Ummmm-Ummmm-Ummmm. Shit girl! Suck that motherfucker! Damn; I want that pussy now baby! Get up here! Simone removes his dick from her mouth; stands up and looks Cap eye to eye. He reaches down and unzips her jeans then slid them off. Ummm-Ummm-Ummm.

Look at that pretty red ass; lawd have mercy on me! Ha-ha-ha. You like that ass soldier! Yes lawd! Smack! He smacks the right cheek with his right hand as the two stood there chest to chest. I'm ready for that pussy baby; turn around for me. Oh yeah; you sure about that Captain!

Shut up and turn around woman. He grabs her by the waist; spins her around and pulls her naked ass up against his penis; bends down and kisses Simone softly on her neck.

Ahhh-Ahhh. That's my spot; I'm so wet right now baby. I like it nice and wet baby. He slides his hand around front and cuffs her pussy then massages her clit with the index finger. Simone's vagina was getting wetter and wetter by the stroke; her pussy started making the smacking sound as her lips open and closed from her pulsating hormones.

Oh God, stop playing with it and put something in it, please! Jeron grabs her by the back of the neck and bends her over; Simone's hands falls down to the coffee table as her ass and pussy sat up spread eagle in front of Cap. He placed one hand on each cheek; spread them apart so that her pussy opened wider then slowly shoved his black love inside her womb.

Uhhh-Uhhh-Uhhh. Harder baby, harder, fuck me harder!Oh yeah; you want hard! He sped up the pace and begun stroking harder and faster; a smacking sound sounded off as his nuts smacked her wet pussy at the end of every stroke. Smack! Smack! Oh-yeah, oh-yeah, oh-yeah! That's it baby! Oh-yeah, oh-yeah! Fuck that pussy! Oh-God-yeah! Uhhhhh-Uhhhhh. Fuck that pussy baby! Fuck it! Uhhh-Hmmm! Give me that pussy! Take it Soldier, take it!

Skkkrrreeeet! Skkkreeeettt! The coffee table slid across the waxed tiled floor as he thrust harder and harder. Oh yeah! That's it! Take this dick baby! Give it to me baby! Give it to me! Oh-yeah! Oh-yeah! Oh-God-Yeah! I'm cumin baby! Get that nut baby! Get it! I got it Cap!

Ummmm-Ummmm-Ummmm. She moans and groans as her body slowly succumbs to a long awaited orgasm then lays her head down on the table.

Jeron got down on his knees and crawled up behind her while she was lying on the table; her pussy was still dripping wet when he went in tongue first. Simone's swollen pussy lips protruded out from behind as he started to lick them. Ummm-Ummm-Ummmm.

That feels good baby; you trying to get me hooked nigga! Ummm-Ummm. Don't stop though baby; damn; your ass is going to be trouble. You nasty motherfucking freak; I like your freaky ass. Put it in my butt whole baby; please I want it inside me! Oh yeah; you want me to bust it open for you baby! Yeah baby; come on; do it!

Uhhhhh-Uhhhhh! She screamed when he slid his thumb in her ass hole. I got to get it loose baby so I can slide it in. Fuck that baby; put it in now; I can take it! Alright! He removed his thumb then slid his hard Johnson in Simone's asshole. Ohhhhhh-

God! Ohhhhh-God! Push it baby! Push it! Ohhhh-God! Ohhhh-God! Fuck that ass baby! Fuck it! Jeron stroked In and out, in and out then in and out for the next several minutes.

Her asshole opened wider as she begun to tremble from the penetration and another orgasm dawned. Ohhhhhhhh! Fuck! Yes! Yes! Yes! You the man nigga! Yes! Woooohhh! Ha-ha-ha. Damn; you a freak too huh baby; talking about me. Ha-ha-ha. Maybe a little! Ha-ha-ha. They both giggle then lay there beside one another on the cold floor.

Ring-Ring-Ring. Damn telephone; who is it now! Cap gets up off the floor and answers the phone. Hello! Cap what's up bruh! Hey Tim; I'm chillin now, what's up? Did that chic ever come by? Who? Simone man! Oh yeah; she's here now.

My man, want you get her sisters number for me! Hold on LT! Hey baby; it's Tim; he wants Tonya's number. Ha-ha-ha. That's funny because she told me to give it to him. No shit! Yep! Hey bruh; hold on a minute. Alright! You got a pen? Yep! Simone tells Cap the number and he relays it to Tim. It's 212-675-9090! Cool thanks man; tell Simone I said hi. Yeah ok; bye man. Click! The two hang up the phone.

Ring-Ring-Ring. Hello; thanks for calling West Coast Image; how may I help you? Yes; can I speak to Tonya please! Sure; hold on please. Hi this is Tonya! Well how the fuck are you lady! Who is this! The guy you fucked and left at the club the other night! Ohhhhhh, hey sweet heart! I am so sorry; let me explain! Please do! Ok, first I want to apologize for being rude; I should have told you I was leaving; will you accept my apology? Why should I?

I mean; you don't have to honey; I was only being nice! That was some bitch shit you did! I said I was sorry! Why did you do it? My crazy ass husband owns the club; he knew we were there celebrating Simone's birthday and sent a car to pick me up.

Damn, Tonya you could have told me you were married! That's fucked up; then the nigga owns the club too. I see you're trying to get my ass shot huh! Nah honey; he and I are not even sleeping in the same room! That fool is a damn ho!

He knows I do my own thing; he doesn't like it but I caught him cheating so many times it's ridiculous. Well I'm glad you told me the whole story because I was feeling some kind of way about how you handled things. I'm sorry honey; let me make it up to you! Oh yeah; how are you planning on doing that? I have tickets to the Knicks game tonight and they're playing the Bulls; front row seats too. No shit!

No shit honey, you wanna come or what? Sure! Great I have to pick up my sisters kids and I can meet you in the front of MSG around 7:00pm. Cool, I will see you then sexy. Great honey; I can't wait to see you again; I want some more of that stick too! Ha-ha-ha. Oh, you can get it sexy; see you later! Bye baby!

Sonya! Yes Ma'am! Call Milton and tell him to hold two of our front row seats at the garden tonight; he can sell the other three. Yes Ma'am; calling him now! Thanks babe! No problem boss! I'm headed home for today; make sure you get all those casting appointments set.

Tonya grabs her long black leather coat from the coat rack and slips it on over her white turtle neck sweater, blue jeans and black leather knee high boots. I have everything set for the castings; I'm only waiting on the two male models to confirm their appointments. Ok, cool; you can leave for today once that's done. Bye girl; see you tomorrow! Have a good night boss!

Tonya walks out of the agency and heads out to pick up the kids. Sonya picks up the office phone to make a call. Ring-Ring-Ring. Yeah who's speaking! Hi Craig; what are you doing? Hey Sonya; I'm just finishing up this meeting over in Harlem; how you doing? I'm great daddy; your wife just left; are you coming by so I can suck that dick? Girl you crazy; I'll be there in 45 minutes; is the receptionist still there? She's leaving as we speak. Cool, I'll see you in a few then; hey; order me some shrimp with lobster sauce from the Red Wall. Ok daddy; you want egg rolls too.

Yeah let me get two veggie rolls. Sure it's a done deal; see you when you get here. Ok love! Bye daddy! Click! The two hang up the phone.

Sonya went to lock the office door after the receptionist left for the day then she took her purse and went to the restroom. Once inside; she removed her short green dress by sliding it down from her shoulders and stepped out of it as it hit the floor. Tonya's assistant looked at herself in the mirror and admired her naked body; her light skin complexion and silky black hair resembled the likes of Sade'.

She massaged her breast for a second then rubbed her hands over her pussy and pulled the lips back to reveal her clit. Sonya softly began to hum a tune to her-self as she reached in her purse to get her lingerie. One red frizzle top and a red frizzled bottom with the crouch open was her outfit of choice. The assistant removed her shoes and slipped on the crouchless red bottoms then the red frizzled top to match; reached down in her purse and retrieved a tube of red lipstick then slowly but softly applied it to her sexy lips then she picked up the cordless office phone.

Ring-Ring-Ring. Hi Red Wall; dine in or carry out! An Asian voice spoke on the other end. Carry out! Go ahead with your order! Can I have a number 17 with shrimp fried rice and a large shrimp with lobster sauce and two veggie egg rolls? Ok; I got a number 17; shrimp fried rice and a shrimp with lobster sauce and two veggie rolls. Yes Ma'am! Ok; your total 25 dollar; what your address? Oh it's 162, 5th Ave.; suite 508; West Coast Image. Thank you; it will be 45 minutes! Thank you!

Ring-Ring-Ring. Hello; West Coast image; how can I help you? Hi this is Mark; I was calling to confirm the casting for the video shoot. Hi Mark I got you signed up; did you speak with Keith? Yeah he's over here shooting pool right now; did you want to speak with him. Yes please! Hold on! Hey Keith; phone dawg! Hello; this is Keith! Hey Keith this is Sonya over at the agency; are you going to be able to make the casting tomorrow? Oh shit; I forgot; yeah count me in.

Alright I got you signed up; thanks baby; you guys have a good evening. You too Sonya! Later! Click! She hangs up the phone and dims the office lights then turns on the cd player. Keith Sweat's; Right and Wrong way was the track she selected. "You're mine, mine, mine, mine" "I'm gonna love you right, girl" "You may be young but you're ready (ready to learn)" "You're not a little girl, you're a woman (take my hand)".

Knock-Knock-Knock. Sonya runs to get the door. It was Craig. Hi daddy! Hey baby;

damn; you look good as fuck in that Victoria secret! Thank you baby and this is Fredrick's; not Victoria. My bad baby; you still killing it though; I want that ass. Right now!

Craig rushed in the door; picked Sonya up and walked her into his wife's office, as they were French kissing each other she fell back on Tonya's desk. Craig removed his arms and in one swoop motion; knocked all the items off the desk onto the floor. He then opened her legs and discovered the crouchless panties.

Damn; that's what the fuck I'm talking about baby! Open wide and let me kiss those pretty lips! You like that daddy; I got them just for you! Hell yes; you always know what I like baby. He placed his hand on her stomach and gently pushed her back on the desk; she took her right hand and slid her pussy lips open so that he could lick the inside like she liked it.

Ummm-mmm. Yeah open that pretty thing up baby; my sweet thang. Sonya picks up the remote that was still lying on the corner of the desk and turned up the cd player. Keith Sweat's; In the Rain was on the player. "I don't wanna cry, I don't wanna cry" "I'm going out in the rain, yes".

The lights were dim; Keith Sweat was on the radio and Sonya was ready to go all in for this night of forbidden passion. Craig slowly licked her vagina from the bottom to the top then back down while licking the insides of her sugar walls. Oooohhhh-yesss! Do it again daddy! He obliged and proceeded to lick up one side; around the clit then back down the other side.

Ooooohhh! Oooooohhh!Oooooohhh! Fuck me daddy! Fuck me! He dropped his hands from her inner thighs and unzipped his slacks; pulled out his dick while he was still eating her pussy. She arched her back up off the desk then let out a loud moan as he stuck his penis inside her juice box. Hmmmmmm!

Damn; you sneaky bastard! Oh God that feels so good! "Now I, I think I'm gonna cry (cry)" "Now I, I don't want you to see me cry". In the midst of their moment a loud voice interrupted their love scene. What the fuck! You bitch! Oh shit! Baby wait! Baby-don't! Shut the fuck up Craig! No baby! Pow! Pow!

Two shots let off from Tonya's gun. Sonya! You slut; get the fuck out! I'm sorry Tonya! Shut up bitch; your ass is fired! Craig you sorry piece of shit! All that pussy out there and you had to fuck my assistant; you sorry ass nigga! Then yall slack asses gonna fuck on my desk; in my motherfucking office! Baby I'm sorry! Don't baby me nigga; go home and get your shit out of my house! But-but-but! But my ass; bye nigga!

She points the gun at him. Ok baby; calm down; I'm going! Craig pulls up his slacks, runs out of the office and passes by Sonya as she was running down the hallway half naked with clothes in hand.

The cold winter air filled the office through the large whole Tonya shot in the window as she sat there on the top of her desk all alone. Tears began to pour from her eyes from the aftershock of what just happened then she pulled herself together; opened the desk drawer and retrieved the cell phone that she originally came for in route to MSG.

Tonya wiped the tears from her eyes; closed the office door; went to the restroom to redo her make-up and headed to the garden. She placed her nine back in her purse turned off the office lights and slammed the door. Bam!

3, New Beginnings.

The scene on base was getting rowdy; it was the day of the annual Army vs. Navy football game; cadets and officers alike were gearing up for this celebrated union. West Point Alumni filled the campus and joined in on the annual tailgating events.

Meanwhile; inside Captain Jeron Briggs office; Lt. Blackburn sat there alongside the MP's in hand cuffs as the officers awaited for the LT's orders for Leavenworth. Cap was just signing the orders when Lt. Blackburn spoke up. Excuse me sir! Yes LT, what is it? How long will I be in Leavenworth? Well LT, you have some serious charges here sir; drug trafficking carries a 5 year mandatory sentence. But Cap; I only have 45 days left before I ETS; how is it I have to do 5 years?

I officially want be in the military once I ETS! LT; you're doing every bit of that time soldier and without pay because you committed the crime while you were enlisted. Man that's some bullshit Cap! Hey; you should of thought about that when you were trying to be a kingpin! LT hung his head down and started to cry at the bad news. Cap finished signing his orders and sent him on his way. Here you go officers; take this soldier to his new home. No problem sir; right away sir! Let's go LT! The MP's lifted the handcuffed soldier to his feet and started him on his perp. walk to the MP's Hum V.

Ring-Ring-Ring. Hello, this is Captain Briggs. Hey Cap, this is Tim; what's going on brother? Nothing much bruh; just sent Blackburn to the brig. Damn; I bet he hated that shit huh? Yep! Anyway what's the word on Tonya man; yall hook up again? Man we went to the Knicks, Bulls game the other day; chic had front row seats too bruh. She got it like that LT?

I guess so Cap; she runs a model agency in the city; has three or four kids and is married to the guy that owns that club we met them at a few weeks ago. Damn; be careful LT? Yeah but they're separated; she just kicked him out the other night. Sounds like your girl got some issues LT; if they're separated; why she had to kick him out; dude shouldn't have been there anyway.

She said they only did it for the kids until she walked in her office the other day and caught him fucking her assistant on her office desk. Damn that nigga is ignorant for that shit LT; her damn assistant! Really! Yeah bruh; I agree! Well; I will meet you at the Officer's club after work; we need to talk about that package. Aright; later Cap!

Cap hangs up the phone and dials Simone's number. Ring-Ring-Ring. Hello! Hey sexy; how are you doing today? Hi baby; I'm good; how are you? Ok I guess; what are you doing tonight around 9 o'clock? Nothing but watching my bad ass kids! Ha-ha-ha. They can't be that bad baby! Shit; just wait, you'll see! Anyway why you ask? I wanted to take you to the BBD concert in the city. Wow! Are you serious baby? Yes I am! What time do I need to be ready? Ha-ha-ha. How about 7:45; we can grab a bite to eat before the concert. Great; that sounds like a plan; I will see you later then baby! Ok sexy! Click! The two hang up the phone.

Knock-Knock-Knock. Come in; it's open! Hey Cap! Hi Gracie; what's up? I just got my new orders today! Good for you; where are you headed? Cap they got me going to Fort Drum; I wanted to go back overseas! Gracie; you know how that works; you go where we need you. Man this is some bullshit; aint a damn thing up there at Fort Drum; I'm going to be bored out of my mind!

Ha-ha-ha. You're probably right; hope you like to drink; that's about all you can do after work besides going to Canada or Niagara Falls on the weekend. That shit aint funny Briggs! I know baby; when do you have to report?

I have 90 days left! Jeron got up from his desk and walked over to his liquor cabinet;

pulled out two glasses; added a few ice cubes and poured them both a drink of Makers Mark. Here you go LT; have a drink; take your mind off of it for a minute. Thanks Cap! Ahhh; don't mention it; you might as well get used to it!

Ha-ha-ha. You got a ton of jokes today Sir! You know I'm just giving you a hard time Gracie! He stands up and she follows then they both toast before taking a drink. Here's to Ft. Drum, 10th Mountain Division! They clash glasses and drink up.

On the serious side LT; you will be fine; it's not that bad. Yeah I guess not; I'm only there for a year anyway. See that's the spirit; well I have to go meet Tim to discuss some business; good luck to you and make sure you come by and see me before you transfer! Of course Cap; you know I want leave without saying goodbye. Alright then; enjoy the rest of your day LT.

They both turn up their glasses to finish their drinks; slams the cups down on the desk then Gracie exits the office; turns around and salutes Cap as she walks away. Briggs; pours himself another drink; turns it up then slams the glass down on his desk; puts on his over coat and heads out to meet Tim.

The entire base was swarming with formations marching to and from their destinations; dependent's and alumni alike drove their cars at a slow pace throughout the base blowing horns and yelling out; GO ARMY! Captain Briggs jumped in his Hum V and drove slowly pass the cadet formations on his way to the officers club. A sea of green covered the base; soldiers in battle dress uniforms, dress greens and Go Army flag's was at every turn.

Cap reached his destination and parked his vehicle in front of the club; several young cadets passing the officers club salute him as they walked by. He acknowledged them and salutes back. You could hear the Army band practicing in the back ground amongst the busy activities.

Jeron walks in the O club; male and female officers alike from LT's to General's crowded the local watering hole. Dull grey marble floors covered the entire building; stained wood panel covered the walls that held pictures of the chain of command; all the way up to the Commander in Chief.

One huge bar sat in the center of the building and formed a square with bar stools on all four sides. Four Bartender's worked the entire bar; one on each side. Hey Briggs! Briggs! Cap heard someone call his name and stops to see who it was; over on the far end of the bar sat LT; Tim Walker. Briggs spots him and walks over to where he is sitting. Hey bro; how was your day at the office? Man it was ok; nothing out of the ordinary Cap.

That's what's up; all is normal on the home front. Shit; normal is good right! Hell yeah! What you drinking LT? I'm on that Crown today bruh! Cool! Briggs waves the bartender over. How you doing Ma'am; can I have a double shot of Crown for the gentleman and a double shot of Smirnoff for me! Yes Sir; coming right up! So Cap; what's the deal on that situation? Oh man; you're not going to believe this shit! Go ahead, try me! Here you are sir; one double Crown and one double Smirnoff! Thanks! Will you be paying now sir or will you like to start a tab? Put it on my tab baby! Ok sir; no problem.

Briggs takes a seat at the bar beside Tim; puts his right hand on his shoulder and the other on his drink. Go ahead Cap; spit it out bruh. Long story short; the MP's fucked up the entire investigation! How's that? This fool Blackburn was speeding on base and got stop by the MP's. When the two officers went to talk to him; they smelled marijuana coming from the car.

Blackburn's crazy ass was high as hell; they found a blunt in the ash tray that he smoked earlier. The MP's asked can they search the vehicle; this nigga says yes! Anyway they search all in the front seat; back seat; under the seats; glove box; every damn thing but didn't find anything. He blurts out; see I told you pussies I didn't have nothing; but this little piece of blunt. He goes on to say. I'm getting out in less than two months and yall can't do a damn thing to my black ass; now what!

The MP's, grew frustrated, took his keys and pulled him out of the car and asked if he could open the trunk. He said; of course. The two officers open the trunk and find three military issued duffle bags full of money that came to a total amount of $500,000.00! What the fuck! Yes the fuck! So where is the money? It's locked up at my headquarters; he was one of my soldiers so they turned it over to me; plus; I'm the highest ranking C.O on base over the MP's.

Let me get this straight Cap! You got half a million dollars stashed away at your office? That is affirmative LT! God damn! So what's the move now; you can't make the bust if he's already locked up; he can't buy the weed from the supplier. Fuck that weed LT; I'm holding on to the money; you and I can open up our own restaurant when we get out! Tim stands to his feet; holds his drink up in the air and clashes glasses with Cap. Hey; that sounds like a plan to me motherfucker! Alright then don't mention this to anyone; I'm going to put the money up for safe keeping for the next three months.

Man; I aint saying a damn thing to nobody! Hey baby! Briggs; wave the bartender back over. Yes sir! Another round please! Sure sir; no problem! I'm leaving after this drink LT; I'm taking Simone to the BBD concert in the city. Cool; that's what's up Cap! Here's your drinks sir! Thanks baby; go ahead and close me out. Sure; no problem. The two officers pick up their drinks and make a toast. Here's to a new life after Uncle Sam! Hell yeah! Cheers! They slam their drinks back, put down the glasses and walk away from the bar then head out to their vehicles.

All was dark inside MSG arena; three blue beams of light shined down on center stage; clouds of white smoke blew in from both sides of the platform. White sparkles danced across the edge of the stage in front of the 1st row; where Jeron and Simone were sitting. "La da da da da da da" "La da da da da da da da da Oh ho". The music started playing as three silhouettes rose up from the floor under the blue beams of light then the voices sing out.

"Tears I see drop from your eyes" "Tell me why you cry". Yayyy! Yayyy! The crowd goes wild. What's up New York City! Yall ready to party tonight! Yayyy! Yayyy! "Guilt I feel when you look at me" "Did I let you down". Simone stood up and pulled Jeron up with her; he wrapped his hands around her waist and pulled her in close from behind. Thank you baby; this is so nice. You're welcome, gorgeous; anything for my baby. Awwww, thank you!

They both started singing along with the artist. "Tell me when will I see you smile again" "Cause I know I messed up, baby (oh)" "And I know you're fed up (ooh), sugar (Hey, hey)". Smile again, Smile again! Ok Simone; you're getting ahead of yourself. Ha-ha-ha. That's my song baby! Come on New York; sing along with us if you know the words! Let's go yall!

The entire arena stands up and sings along. "Promises I know I made many times before" "And I broke each one of them" "But I had to learn over and over again" "Don't hurt the one you love". Yeah New York! That's it! Are there any lovers in the house tonight! The crowd screams. Yeaaaahhhhh! Ok then; we're gonna take you guy's on a love ride with us tonight! Can we do that New York! Yeaaaahhhhh! Yeah yall ready for that! Fellas grab your ladies and hold them tight and enjoy the music baby! "On a perfect day, I know that I can count on you" "When that's not possible" "Tell me can you weather the storm".

45 minutes had passed and the concert was nearing its end; Simone was now sitting on Jeron's lap, he caressed her gently from

behind while holding his warm face against hers. The artist had just finished their last song for the night. New York City we had a great time with yall tonight. Thanks for all the love; have a good night and may God bless you all! Clap-Clap-Clap. The crowd stands to applause, a perfect end to a romantic night.

It's now Sunday evening and Tonya and the kids are at her Mom's for dinner over in Long Island. Hey kids, come eat! Tonya and Simone yelled out to the children; so they could come downstairs to eat dinner. Their parents are down south for the winter visiting relatives. Simone sat at one end of the table and her sister at the other. So sis; how was the concert the other night? Girl I had a ball, Jeron was all over me the entire time. Whaaaatttt, I know you liked that bitch.

Hell yeah; aint nothing like a man holding you tight and kissing on your neck. Mommy! Mommy! Yes baby! Can we have some tea? Yeah baby, now sit down so you guys can eat. Tonya gets up from the table and walks over to the fridge to get the tea. Simone gets up and places eight plates on the table. Hey Tonya; can you get that garlic bread out of the oven please? Yes Ma'am!

Simone takes the lid off of the large silver pot that was in the center of the table. She picks up the serving spoon and fills each plate with some spaghetti noodles from the pot then covered them with ground beef and Prego.

Tonya placed the pitcher of tea on the counter then removed the garlic bread from the oven and took it over to the table. Thank you sis! No problem babe! Tonya then filled eight glasses with sweet tea and took them over to the table as well.

Yay! We got spaghetti! Ok, ok, calm down kids, it's time for dinner. Everyone sat down at the table and started to eat. Soooooo, Sis! Yes; what is it Tonya? How are things with you and Jeron? Things are good; he's a real cool guy. How about you and Tim?

Well after we talked about my situation with the ex; we're all good. That's what's up; I'm glad you kicked your ex out; that nigga wasn't no good! Girl who you telling; nothing but drama! Did you hire a new assistant yet? Nah; I'm putting an ad out in the Voice next week. Sonya was so wrong for that shit; how could she fuck her boss's husband.

Simone shook her head after she made the comment and picked up a fork of spaghetti. Sis I don't even want to think about it; I should of capped that bitch but I got the kids to think about you know. Yeah; you did the right thing girl; don't even sweat it. Child I aint even thinking about his ass; pass me that parmesan cheese please. Sure! Simone reaches to the left of her to get the cheese and hands it to her niece. Here pass that to your mom sweetie! Ok auntie!

Here you go mommy! Thanks baby! Knock-Knock-Knock! Who the hell is that at my door? Are you expecting someone Simone, they're knocking pretty hard girl!

Simone gets up from the table and walks in the living room to look through the curtain. She slides the white shear curtain back that was covering the oblong window beside the front door. Hell nah! Bitch it's your fucking husband! What! Yep and his ass looks drunk as hell too; clothes hanging off his butt! Tonya now filled with anger; walks to the door. Simone opens the front door.

Craig what the hell do you want nigga; with your trifling ass! Tonya; come get this fool before he falls and bust his ass on these steps. Sis I swear you be picking them sorry red ass niggas! Simone walks off and leaves the couple to iron out their situation. Kids finish your food and stop playing' don't make me get my belt! Sit down! The kids had become restless and wanted to leave the table so they could play Nintendo. If you guys don't finish your spaghetti, there will be no rice crispy treats! Ok-Ok!

The kids screamed then sat back down to finish dinner. Yeah that's what I thought now finish up. Tonya stands at the door shouting. Craig; come in the house; why are you here anyway? Craig walked up the six icy steps in front of the Long Island home; Tonya grabs him by the hand and helps him inside.

The couple; walks over to the living room and take a seat beside each other on the brown leather sofa. Baby I just had to see you; I want to come back home. Nigga kiss my ass; you must think I'm a fool! Baby I'm serious; please forgive me. Hell no! Get out! Get out now; sorry motherfucker! You gone fuck my employee and try and ask me to forgive you!

Smack! Smack! Tonya slapped him twice against his head with an open hand. Damn baby! Why you do that! Shut up and get out Craig! Daddy! Daddy! Hey baby girl! Their youngest daughter had come around the corner into the living room and ran to her Daddy's arms. Muah! Muah! He kisses his daughter and picks her up from the floor.

Tonya is standing there holding the door open awaiting for him to exit. Ok baby; tell daddy bye, bye! Bye Daddy! Bye baby girl! He puts her down then Tonya pushes him in the back to force him out the door. Hey Bitch! Who you calling Bitch! Smack! She slaps him in the head again. Thump! Craig pushes her in the chest and her back slams against the door.

Hey what the hell is going on out here! Simone came up front after she heard the loud thump. This fool gone put his hands on me sis! What! Simone goes in her purse that was sitting on the coffee table and pulls out her 22.

Tonya stands there yelling at Craig. Yeah; now what nigga; push me again! Simone had made it over to the door; then without saying a word. Pow! Pow! Oh shit, what you doing girl! I'm gone pop your ass if you touch my sister again nigga! Ok-Ok! Get out of my yard; the next time; I promise I want miss! I'm gone, I'm gone!

He walks away fast and mumbles under his breath. Damn crazy ass sisters; I don't know why I ever married that crazy fool and her sister. Close the door Tonya; you need to call the police and put a restraining order on that fool. Girl for what; that boy aint gone do nothing! You never know sis; better to be safe than sorry. I'm good sis, that won't be necessary. The sisters make their way back into the kitchen.

The kids had all finished their food. Awwwww; yall cleaned your plates! Good job kids; now put your dishes in the sink and we will fix you guys some dessert while you're playing Nintendo. Mommy where did daddy go? The twins asked Tonya.

Boys your daddy had to leave, you can call him later, ok! Ok mommy! The kids left the table and came up front to the living room where the TV was. Ok Darnell, turn on the Nintendo and you guys take turns, ok. Yes Ma'am.

Tonya left them upfront and returned to the kitchen table with Simone. Girl what are you going to do about that fool husband of yours? Sis, can we talk about something else please! Sure! Shit; I need a drink! Where does Dad keep his stash? Tonya asked Simone then got up from the table. Ha-ha-ha! Look in the cabinets over the fridge; there's a bottle of Crown in there, I think. Girl how do you know that? You've been hitting the stash?

Yes! Ha-ha-ha! We got to get another bottle tomorrow because this is not gonna last tonight. Tonya reaches in the cabinet and pulls out the purple bag. Simone starts putting the dishes in the dish washer and wiping down the stove, counter and kitchen table. Tonya takes two glasses from the cabinet adds a few cubes of ice in each, pours in some crown and tops them with some ginger ale.

She takes the drinks over to the kitchen table and haves a seat, Simone finishes up her cleaning and joins her sister. You know

Tonya; I've been trying to call Jason's punk ass for two weeks. This nigga aint even sending me no child support or nothing! Hell; he aint even seen Tameka yet and Tara is asking for his ass almost every night! Sis; fuck that nigga! You don't need him; he aint no good for you no way! I know but how can you not even take the time to see your baby girl! Really Tonya! He doesn't even know how she looks! Simone, I know it's hard but it's for the best sis. All you guys ever did was fight; how many times did that fool give you a black eye?

He's lucky daddy didn't kill his ass girl. Remember that time yall were staying in California and he had that bitch in yalls bed while you were at work? That nigga aint no good; so stop crying over his ass! I aint crying over that fool sis; I'm just upset that he's not trying to be a part of his daughters lives. That's a selfish motherfucker baby and God is going to make sure he gets what's coming to him.

I know sis; I'm just tired of trying to find a man that will treat me like Dad treats Mom. Every time I think I've finally found him; he don't be about shit! Simone you just have to keep praying baby and don't give up hope. Yeah I know sis, it's just frustrating that's all. Tonya looks at her sister; touches her hand then speaks softly. Hey, why don't you have a drink with me little sis. Simone smiles; lifts her head and speaks. Shit, make mine a double!

You got it bitch! Girl we have to get dad another bottle before they get back. I will pick one up on my way to the agency tomorrow. Simone opens the bottle and pours the remaining contents into their glasses. Knock-Knock-Knock. Mommy someone's at the door! Ok Darnell, go look through the window and see who it is. Ok! Little Darnell runs to the window and slides back the curtain.

Mommy it's Aunt Lisa! Ok let her in honey! He unlocks the dead bolt and let her in. Hey there handsome! Muah! Lisa picks up

Darnell and gives him a big juicy kiss. Hey Auntie! Lisa was a large woman, she stood 5'5" and wore somewhere around 280 lbs.

Her gorgeous black silky hair fell to her shoulders and draped around her cute fat face. When she spoke, she spoke softly and had the biggest heart but didn't take any shit from no one, especially her husband. Hey Lisa! We're in the kitchen baby! Tonya yelled out.

Ok baby! Lisa closes the door behind her; puts down Darnell and walk over to the living room to speak to the rest of the kids. Hey cutie pies, what are you guys doing? Hey Aunt Lisa, we're playing Nintendo! I see! Are you guys having fun? Yes Ma'am!

Come give Auntie a hug! The kids jump off the couch and run to give their Aunt a hug. Ok, thank you babies, I'm going to talk to your moms, ok. Ok! The kids run back to the couch and continue playing their game. Lisa makes her way into the kitchen. Hey, what you ho's in here doing?

Hey girl, we just having a drink; what you doing today? Girl I had to get out of the damn house, my damn husband done pissed me off. Damn, what did Scotty do now Lisa? Simone, this nigga gone lose all of our rent money playing some motherfucking poker! What the fuck, you got to be kidding me! I wish I was Tonya! Did you beat his ass again girl. I whipped that fool like he stole something; gave his ass two black eyes! I should have broken his got damn legs but he has to work!

I swear that skinny nigga gets on my nerves! Shit I'm surprised he aint left you yet; much as you beat his ass! Girl that fool aint going anywhere; he likes when I beat him up. Ha-ha-ha! Whatever bitch! You crazy!

Lisa takes a seat at the table with the sisters and pulls out a pack of Virginia Slims cigarettes from her bra; takes one out and lights it. So what's new over here with yall two? Same drama girl, we we're just talking about Craig's trifling ass. Oh what ever happen with that Tonya? Did you kick his ass out?

Hell yeah; that fool came over here about an hour ago trying to make up. Stop your lying girl! I'm serious, he was all drunk and shit; Simone had to let off two caps so that fool could leave! What! Yall had some drama over here this morning. Did that fool run girl? Ha-ha-ha. Like a mutt with his tail between his legs. Simone you my bitch girl! Tonya, what are you gonna do with that fool girl? I'm fed up Lisa; I'm filing for a divorce next week and get this thing over with. Good because it will only get worse. Where's the Crown at? You knuckle heads done drunk it all up huh? Yep!

Lisa stands up. Hey where are you going girl? Calm down Tonya, I'll be right back! I got a bottle of rum in the car. Oh shit, it's on now baby. Shut up Simone; you alcoholic. Whatever Lisa, hurry your ass up. Tonya gets up from the table and walk over to the counter to cut the rice crispy treats.

You want one Simone? Yeah, just a small piece! Ok!

Tonya cuts several squares of the treats and a small one for her sister and puts them on 9 paper saucers. Hey kids; come get your dessert! Here you go sis! She hands Simone hers. The kids run in the kitchen to get their plates. Ok, you guys can take it back in the living room with you; don't get any on your Grandma's couch. Ok mommy! Ok Auntie!

The kids take their treats and run back into the living room. Lisa walks back inside with a bottle of Bacardi. Alright bitches; let's party! Simone gets an extra glass out of the cabinet for Lisa and adds a few cubes of ice.

The ladies all have a seat at the table. So bitches what's been going on with them two soldiers yall picked up at the club the other night? Girl we good, those two niggas got their shit together; huh sis! Slap! Simone gave her sister a high five. Well tell me all about it! Did yall get some dick finally? Shit child Tonya's slut ass fucked

Tim at the club that night! What! You whore! Hey whatever girl; I had to get me some! Simone went on base and got her back knocked out in the barracks! Damn Simone; you drove on base to get that dick girl?

Hell yeah; you good over there with your husband; we need to get it when we can and the best we can! Amen! BAM! Tonya slams her hand down on the kitchen table. You can say that again sis! Ha-ha-ha! All three ladies laugh loud and continuously.

Knock-Knock-Knock. Damn, who the hell is it now. Tonya gets up from the table to answer the door. She makes her way to the front room. Who is it? Hey it's Scotty; is my wife here? She opens the door to let him in then yells out to Lisa. Lisa it's your husband! Scotty walks in wearing a pair of shades and holding a bouquet of flowers. She's in the kitchen Scott. He makes his way into the kitchen where Lisa and Simone are sitting; Tonya follows.

Baby, what are you doing here! I came to say I'm sorry. Lisa stands up and looks at him; Scott is standing there at the end of the table and the ladies are all staring at him with amusement and aw. Why should I even listen to you baby; you keep fucking up! I know, I know but I am serious Lisa. I aint got time for this! Here honey these are for you; just listen ok!

Scott hands her the flowers; removes his shades then unzips his blue jump suit that he wore when he worked as a mechanic. A frail gentlemen wearing around 115 pounds; 5 foot 2 and brown skinned the total opposite of his wife. Damn! Your eyes are fucked up buddy! Ha-ha-ha. Shut up Simone; leave my baby alone. Scott reaches in his inside pocket and pulls out a wad of cash then placed it on the table. What is that baby? This is the rent honey; I fixed three cars today. Oh shit Lisa; your hubby stepping up. Tonya; don't even go there! I'm just saying; he got the rent. Yeah! Only because she beat his ass then gave him two black eyes. Ha-ha-ha. Fuck you Simone! Ha-

ha-ha. They all start to laugh at the situation including Scott.

Lisa steps away from the table; pulls her husband by the arm and gives him a huge hug. I love you baby; momma's gonna give you some of this chocolate pudding tonight daddy! Ahhhhh! Get yall's asses out of my kitchen with that mess; go to the bedroom! Hey stop hating Simone! Ha-ha-ha. Come on baby; bye ladies! Lisa and Scott grabbed each other's hand and headed for the front door.

Ring-Ring-Ring. Tonya takes the telephone headset from the wall. Hello! Damn! Hey Tonya; watch that damn cord girl; you almost choked me! Tonya stops and goes the other way so that the telephone cord wouldn't be in Simone's way. Hello! Hey sexy; what you doing? Hey Tim! Nothing much; just sitting over here with Simone and the kids. That's what's up. What are you doing? I'm over at Jeron's having a drink. Oh yeah, what are you guys sipping on? Baby we're on that black rum right now.

Don't get too drunk now Mr.! I'm good; I know my limit. You better! Hey; what are you and Simone doing later? Not a damn thing, what's up? You guys should meet us later so we can go check out that new movie? What movie? That new one, Menace II Society! Oh, that Gangster shit; hold on! Tonya puts the phone down. Hey sis, you want to go see Menace II Society tonight? Girl, who are we going with? Tim and Jeron; this is Tim on the phone now! Well in that case; sure let's do it! Is Jeron with him now? Yes! Simone screams out! Hey Captain! Ha-ha-ha. Sis you silly! He said hi!

Well what time should we be ready? We can be over around nine! Ok see you guys then; I have to call the sitter! Ok; bye baby! Tonya places the phone back on the wall and puts on her jacket. Simone I'll be right back; I'm going next door to see if Lizzy can watch the rug rats. Alright girl; I'll get their things ready. Tonya opens the front door; walks carefully down the slippery steps and through the snow to the neighbors.

Ding-Dong! Come in; it's open! Tonya push open the blue wooden door of the green two storied home then walks inside. Well hello their young lady! A deep, raspy, Irish voice; sing out from a little old woman sitting in a brown lazy boy recliner. A red brick fire place held a small fire that created a large shadow on her plane white walls. Coffee colored carpet covered the front room wall to wall and a huge floor model TV sat in the corner to the left of the fireplace.

Lizzy wore a long blue robe with matching slippers; her pale white skin looked cold to the touch. Her red hair was thinning on the top but was long and pretty falling down to her back. Hi Lizz! Hello Tonya! Come in honey; have a seat.

A light brown couch and love seat sat in the middle of the room and there in the center of them was a large oval maple coffee table. Tonya made her way over to the love seat; it sat closest to Lizzy's recliner. Sweet smelling smoke filled the air around her chair from the cigar that she held in her right hand. You want a drink honey; I have some whiskey on the top shelf. No Ma'am; I wanted to ask if you could watch after the kids tonight. Sure honey; it's no problem bring them on over. Ok; thanks Lizzy; you're the greatest! Don't mention it honey; it's not a big deal. Muah! She kisses her on the cheek and heads back over to her mother's house.

Bam-Bam-Bam! Open this damn door Sonya! Bam-Bam-Bam! Girl what are you doing; open the door! No Craig you're drunk! Bitch; you better open this motherfucking door; before I kick it down. Bam-Bam-Bam! Craig continues to knock on the door, harder and harder. Sonya ran to the door of her duplex and placed a kitchen table chair under the door knob. Go away Craig! Bam-Bam-Bam-Bam!

Damn it Sonya! Go away Craig! Sonya picked up her phone to dial 911. Ring-Ring-Ring. 9-1-1, what's your emergency? Yes my boyfriend won't go away; he's drunk and want go away! Ma'am, do you feel threatened? No, I just want him to go away! Ok, is he still there? Hold on, he stopped knocking. Sonya walked over to peep out of the window to see if Craig was indeed gone. All was quiet and there was no sign of him; she puts the phone back to her ear. Ma'am; he's gone! Ok darling, do you want us to send a unit out?

No Ma'am, it's ok; I'm fine. Well, have a good evening darling; call back if you need us. Thank you; good bye! Click! She hangs up the phone and heads into the kitchen of her Harlem duplex.

Meow-Meow-Meow. Peppa! Sonya shouted when she seen her black and white spotted cat walk across the back porch. She ran to open the back door so Peppa could come in the house. Smack-Smack! Craig; stop! He slapped her in the head when she walked out as he hid on the right side of the doorway. Bitch next time I tell you to open the door; open that shit! Do you hear me?

Yes Dear! He stoops down and picks up Peppa. Hey kitty, kitty; come in the house Sonya and close the door; what you cooking for dinner? Sonya walks in and locks the door behind her; wipes the tears from her eyes then sit on the kitchen counter. I'm sorry baby I didn't want to hit you but you were acting stupid earlier for no damn reason. I'm sorry Craig; I didn't mean to upset you. It's ok baby; just don't do that shit again. What you cooking for dinner? I'm hungry as I don't know what! What do you want baby?

How about, some pork ribs with some mashed potatoes and corn. Sure I can make that. He walks over to Sonya; grabs her gently by the chin and softly kisses her on the lips. Muah! See how easy things can be baby; just do as I say and we won't have any problems. Ok dear.

Sonya takes the ribs from the freezer, potato off the refrigerator door and can of whole kernel corn from the pantry. Honey; grab me a beer while you in the fridge please. Sure! She puts the food on the counter and grabs a beer from the fridge and throws it at him. Bam! What the fuck! The bottle flew pass his head and shattered against the wall. You're trying to hit me with that shit Sonya! No baby, I'm sorry! Here; let me get you another one.

Craig walks over to the counter and took the other beer she handed him. You lucky that didn't hit me girl! I'm sorry honey; it was a mistake. Yeah ok! Ring-Ring-Ring. Answer the phone woman! Man; if you want to eat anytime soon; you need to get it yourself so I can start cooking. Craig walks over by the stove where she is standing. Thump! Stop it Craig! That shit hurt! Ring-Ring-Ring. Thump! He kicks her in the ass again. Get the phone bitch and who the fuck do you think you're talking to! Ring-Ring-Ring. Get the phone! Sonya picks up the phone. Hello!

Yes; is Craig there? Hold on! Here; telephone! Hello; who's speaking? Hi Craig this is Detective Washington; there's been a break in at your club. Shit! Are you serious? Yes sir. Did they take anything? Yep; I'm afraid so sir; you might want to come down here sir. Damn; I'm on the way Detective. He hangs up the phone. Don't worry about that food baby; get your things we're headed down to the club; someone broke in my shit. What! The two of them grab their coats and head down to the club.

4, Baggage.

Tonya, Tim, Simone and Jeron are exiting the movie theater; it's 9:30 pm on a windy New York night in Times Square. So ladies did you guys enjoy the movie? Yeah I did baby; thank you for taking us. Your welcome Tonya; glad you liked it! Hey bruh; I'm hungry; you guys want to come with me and Simone to the Steak House? Man why you asking a crazy question; you know that's my favorite spot! Ha-ha-ha.

I knew that would get your attention; you and Tonya all up under each other over there. Ouch! Come here! Hey! All you had to do was ask Simone; you didn't have to pinch me. I'm sorry did I hurt you Captain! Ha-ha-ha. Whatever; let's go eat! The couples head next door to the Steak House. Two glass doors trimmed in oak wood with Steak House stenciled on the windows dressed the entrance.

Jeron held the doors open for the others then followed them in; once inside the hostess greeted them at the door. Hello; welcome to the Steak House; will we be seating four? Yes Ma'am and can you make sure we're in the non-smoking section. Yes Ma'am; I can do that! Please; follow me to your seats.

The hostess leads the way into the dining area; the others followed. Fresh grilled shrimp; fried eggs; grilled chicken, onions and peppers left a mouth-watering aroma in the air.

12 huge stove top grills covered the dining area; accompanied by 8 Chef's wearing white garments and hats. Dark grey commercial carpet covered the floor, bamboo walls complemented the bamboo trimmed grills and black bamboo chairs. Tonya, Simone, Tim and Jeron follow the hostess to table 6 and occupy the four vacant seats on the left side of the grill. As they take their seats the Chef welcomes them to his table.

Hello ladies and gents; welcome to the Steak House; our special for this evening is Shrimp stir fry with our 16 oz. T-Bone. Ohh yeah; let me get the T-bone, medium rare! Sure Ma'am and what will you be having Ma'am? Honey my name is Simone; you can call my sister Ma'am; I aint that old. Ha-ha-ha. Shut up Simone. What you laughing at Tim? Anyway; let me have the shrimp stir fry sir. Ok ladies, and gents; how about you? I think I'm going to have the steak too; go ahead Tim; he's waiting on your order. Oh!

Tonya and Tim were hugged up and smooching on each other. Let me have the steak too Chef and make that well done. Ok, coming right up folks. The Chef pulled the menu items from his cart and began to prepare their orders on the grill. Ring-Ring-Ring. Tonya cell phone rings. Hold on baby; let me get this. Hello! Hey Tonya! What's up Craig? I'm down at the club, there was a break in. Damn, did they take anything? Yeah; they took a lot of shit! Fuck! Is my Nine still there? Nope, that's why I'm calling; the detective said you need to file it stolen with the police department soon as possible before something happens.

Ok; thanks I will take care of that as soon as I get a chance. Ok, talk to you later Tonya. Alright bye Craig! Click! Damn! What's wrong sis? Someone broke in the club and they stole my gun along with some other shit.

You need to call it in stolen ASAP! Yeah I know Jeron; I'm on it. I need a drink now; where's our waitress? Excuse me! Excuse me! Simone calls out to the waitress as she leaves the adjacent table.

Yes Ma'am; what can I do for you? We like to order some drinks. Sure what can I get you? Baby; start us off with two rounds of tequila; make each one a double too! Ha-ha-ha! Coming right up Ma'am; do you want lemons and salt with it? Yes I do; thank you baby! No problem Ma'am; I will be back in a few with your drinks.

The Chef places the vegetables on the grill, pulls out his knife and starts slicing them for the entrée's. He flips the shrimp so that the other side could sear then slides his fork to the center of the grill to remove the steaks.

Damn that smells good dude! I'm ready to eat! Hold your horses Cap; he's almost done. Simone that boy can eat girl; that steak aint even gone fill him up. Shut up Tim; nobody asked for your two cents.

Ha-ha-ha! Yall be fighting like brothers. Shiiittttt. Tim don't want none; I'll beat him down! Ha-ha-ha! Yeah whatever Cap! Ha-ha-ha. Both guys burst out laughing at the comment. Alright here's your shrimp Ma'am, a steak for you, well done for you and medium rare for you.

Chef places their entrées on the plates that sat in front of them. Thanks Chef! Your welcome sir; enjoy your meal folks. The Chef gather his things and places them on the cart, cleans the grill, turns it off and heads back to the kitchen. The waitress makes her way back over to the table. Ok guys; here's your first round; let me know when you're ready for the second. You can bring them now honey! Ok; I'll be right back!

On the other side of town; Craig and Sonya are sitting at the bar with the detective completing the police report. Ok sir; I need you to take a look around and let me know what's missing so we can include it in the report. Alright! Craig and the Officer get up from the bar and proceed to walk around the club. Hey baby can you fix me a coke; did you want anything detective? Sure can I have a coke also! You got that baby! Yep!

Sonya gets up and walks behind the bar to fix the sodas. Damn; look at this shit! The detective is standing beside Craig with his flash light as they walk up the next level to the V.I.P area while Craig shouts in anger. These stupid fuckers cut up all my damn sofas! Cotton hung out of the deep slashes that were made in the blue chairs and pillows; it looked as if twenty alley cats had got a hold to the furniture and went haywire.

Man I have to replace everything; look; they even broke the tables. Sir; do you have any idea who would do this? Hell nah! Let's go out back and see if anything's out there. The detective follows him out of the emergency exit. As the two gentlemen walk outside they spot a blue Jeep Cherokee about 4 feet from the back entrance with a flat tire. Does this vehicle belong to you or one of your employees? Nah man; I never seen it before! Well this just might be the break we need.

The detective pulls his radio from his hip. This is 74 to base! Go ahead 74! Can you get a CSI unit out to our location; we have a vehicle of interest. Roger that 74, over and out! Roger!

Craig and the detective continue to search the back alley. I don't see anything out here man! Ok let's go inside and finish up the report; they did more damage than anything; didn't really steal nothing; just the Nine and a few bottles of liquor. Yeah this is some bullshit; it's going to take me at least two weeks to get some new furniture; waiting on my insurance company. As they walk inside; Sonya meets them on the dance floor.

Here you go guys! Thanks baby! Thank you Ma'am! You're welcome! I just need for you to sign this report sir and I can get to work on your case. The two gentlemen take a seat at the bar. Just sign right here sir. Craig takes the pen from the officer and signs the report. Thank you; here's your copy! Your welcome and thanks again man. Craig shakes the detectives hand as he stands up. I will give you a call as soon as we find something out! Alright sir; have a good night.

Sonya walks up behind him and starts to massage his shoulders. Ummmm, that feels good baby. I bet it does; you're so tense; I know you're stressed right now. Shit; that aint even the half of it! She continues to massage his neck and tendons then back to his shoulders. Damn baby; I'm getting hard; come around here and give me some of that good head.

He grabs her hands; pulls them off his shoulders and guides her around to the front of him. Ha-ha-ha. Wait baby! Hey where are you going! Sonya giggles and runs away. I'm going to put on some music baby; lock the front door. Craig rise slowly from the bar stool and makes his way over to the main entrance to lock the door. Sonya is up in the Dj booth turning on the sound system. Its locked baby, now come on! Ok hold on; let me put this track on! Yeah here it is.

The music is playing low and they could barely hear it. Turn it up baby; the volume is in the middle of the mix board. Oh I see it! She raises the volume and it's R. Kelly's; Honey Love. Sonya walks down from the Dj booth and back over to Craig at the bar. "There's something in your eyes baby" "It's telling me you want me baby" "Tonight is your night". Yeah this is more like it; give me that dick daddy. Come over here and get it girl; it's ready for you too. Oh yeah. Yep!

"Baby come inside" "Oh, turn down the lights". Sonya reaches down to unzip his pants then pulls her sweater up over her head to reveal her sexy breast and hard nipples piercing through her white wife beater T-shirt. Craig leans back against the bar as she begun to stroke him slowly and gently. You like that daddy; does it feel good to yuh? Hell yeah! Suck it already baby.

She squats down from her standing position and slowly moves her mouth closer to his Johnson. He reaches down and slowly guides it in her mouth pass her red lipstick and sexy lips.

Hmmmm, your mouth is warm baby, it feels so good. She stroked up then back down then back up slowly. Ohhhhh shit, that feels so fucking good. Suck it baby, suck it! He takes both his hands and pulls her hair back to keep it from getting in the way. Hmmm-Hmmm-Hmmm. She moans as she continues to give him that great feeling of ecstasy.

Damn, don't stop; you feel so good baby. Sonya continued to suck on his cock and looked up at him with her pretty brown eyes. Craig stroked her hair gently with both hands then pulled it to the back of her head again then held it in a ponytail. The look in her eyes was sincere and filled with passion and curiosity all at the same time. He lifted her up and guided her towards him; kissed her softly and slowly on the lips then reached under her skirt to remove her panties but she wasn't wearing any. Damn, I like that; no panties huh. None daddy!

Sonya climbed up on top of him as the barstool turned and placed his back against the bar. Ummmm, oh God! She whispered as his dick penetrated her wet vagina. "Give me that honey love" "Give me that honey love" "I got to have your lovin baby".

Skreeeet-Skreeeet! The barstool scraped back and forth over the polished floor as it rocked against the bar. Oh yeah; give me that wet pussy baby; it's so damn juicy! Uhhhh-Uhhhh-Uhhhh! Yes daddy! Yes daddy!Skreet-Skreet-Skreet. Bam!

The barstool fell to the floor as they leaned up against the bar; Craig was now holding her up in the air as she wrapped her legs around his waist. Yes daddy! He squeezed her butt cheeks with every stroke while holding her up by cuffing her ass. Yes daddy! Hit that pussy! Hit it daddy! Ummmph-Ummmph!

He moaned as her juices begin to flow down his nuts and inner thighs. Oh God! Daddy I'm Cumming! Oh God! Oh God! Yes! Yes! Yeeessssss! Craig leaned back against the bar as she slid down from his arms and laid there upon his chest on his soaking wet shirt.

A few days later in the city; its New York fashion week and all is busy over at West Coast Image Modeling agency. Ring-Ring-Ring. Hello, thank you for calling WCI; how may we help you? Yes how are you? I'm fine! That's good; I was calling to speak with my girlfriend! Who's your girlfriend? Oh I'm sorry; that would be Sonya. Sonya! Yes! I'm sorry sir; she is no longer employed here! What; are you sure? Yes I am; would you like to speak with my boss? Yes please! Hold one!

The receptionist puts him on hold and pages Tonya. Tonya I have a gentlemen on line 1! Who is it? He says he's Sonya's boyfriend! Boyfriend! That slut got a nigga! Yeah I'll get it! Hello this is Tonya; I understand that you're looking for Sonya. Yes Ma'am, that is correct. May I ask what it's pertaining to. Well I just got back from Korea on TDY a six month tour and I wanted to surprise her.

Awwwww, how sweet of you! What's your name darling? Oh I'm sorry; my name is

David. Nice to meet you David; well unfortunately I had to let your girlfriend go some time ago. Wow; she didn't even mention that to me when we spoke the other day.

Really; I have no idea why she didn't tell you. Damn, well did she get another job or what? I don't know David. Why did you fire her? Oh, do you really want to know? Yes please! Are you sitting down? I am! Well I walked in one night after work to find her fucking my husband in my office on my desk.

Excuse me! You heard it right David; I didn't stutter. That stinking bitch! Well I had harsher words but those will suffice. I'm sorry I had to tell you the bad news David; I hope you find her soon. She may be at her apartment; don't be surprised if she has a house guest; I kicked my sorry excuse for a husband out of my place after that episode.

Damn' well thank you Tonya and I'm sorry! Why are you apologizing; you didn't fuck my husband; it was your slutty girlfriend. If I was you David, I would keep moving, don't even waste your time going to see that skank! Yeah I hear you but I have some unfinished business with her before I move on. Ok have it your way; take care! Click! Tonya hangs up and gets back to business.

After the incident with Craig and Sonya she fired her receptionist who was referred by Sonya and hired a new secretary and assistant. She paged the front desk. Hey Inga! Yes Ma'am! Do I have any 4pm appointments today? Yes, you have three; the first one walked in about 10 minutes ago. Who is it? It's Darwin from the event planning company. Oh send him back and could you get me some bagels and coffee? Yes Ma'am!

Sir; you can go on back; Tonya will see you now. Thank you! Your welcome sir! The gentleman makes his way to the office. Ding! The elevator door opens and the delivery guy approaches the receptionist. Hello Inga; you're looking sexy today. Thank you; what you got there? Oh it's a dozen red roses for Tonya from some guy name Tim. Ok; I will get them to her. Great; see you next time! Have a good day! The delivery guy gets on the elevator and makes his way back downstairs. Inga goes over to the break area to make Tonya's coffee and toast some bagels.

Ok Darwin; have a seat sir; I will be with you in a second. No problem; take your time Tonya. She walks over to the window and pulls back the blinds. Well let's get started; how's everything looking for Fashion week? Actually, everything looks pretty good, the venue is all set, models are practicing as we speak and the sponsors all met their deadlines. What; are you serious? Yep! So we got all the checks in from our sponsors, all the designers delivered their clothes and the venue is all prepared? Yep! Well good job sir!

Hey; you know I aim to please baby! Knock-Knock-Knock! Come in Inga! The receptionist enters the office with bagel over top of the coffee in one hand and the dozen of roses in other. Wow! Roses! Yep, from Tim!

Awwww, look at you Ms. Thing! Are you blushing over there? Shut up Darwin! Sit the coffee down over here baby; give me the flowers and go look under the cabinet in the break room; there's a vase; put some water in it and bring it back. Ok Ma'am!

So I see you're still getting your groove on miss! Hell yeah, the party don't stop baby! Shit; I'm jealous; now I have to order some for my wife; I'm going to be thinking about that look on your face all day girl. Ha-ha-ha.

Boy you crazy! Did you want some coffee? Yeah sure! How do you like it? Two creams, three sugars! Ok. Tonya picks up the phone and pages Inga. Inga; can you bring another coffee with two creams and three sugars please? Yes Ma'am! So how does the new denim line look this year?

I like it; the jeans for the guys are starting to get baggy now though. Really! Yeah every designer is jumping on the Hip-Hop band wagon!

Yeah they see where the money is; that's why! Not only that; they get free advertising every time one of these rap artist wear their clothes in a video on BET or Mtv! Like I said; they see where the money is!

Tonya picks up the roses and smells them. Ummmm, they are fresh too; this guy may be a keeper. Inga walks back in the office. Here's your coffee sir and where did you want the vase Ma'am? Just sit on the desk baby; thank you. No problem Ma'am!

She sits the vase down and returns upfront to her desk. Do you think we need any more models Darwin; maybe two or three alternates? Yeah; I would have at least two on standby just in case. Yeah; I was thinking the same thing; I will have Inga call two alternates in a bit. Alright; I guess we're all done then. Yep I don't have anything else; let me get back to the office and thanks for the coffee. Ok; bye Darwin see you tomorrow! He gets up, leaves her office and makes his way to the elevator to return to his day.

Tonya places the roses in the vase and picks up the phone to call Tim. Ring-Ring-Ring. Hello this is LT, how can I help you? Hey Tim! Hi baby; did you like them? Yes I did; thank you! Your welcome! So what are your plans for tonight? Nothing much, just going to relax a little, resting up for fashion week. Oh that's cool. Why you ask; what's up baby? I thought maybe we could go get some sushi and hang out a little before you take it in. Sushi; Really!

Yes Ma'am! Damn, you're just full of surprises today aren't you hun? Hey just trying to make sure my baby is happy. Ha-ha-ha. Good answer; well in that case; I can be available around 8pm; how's that? That's perfect baby; I will pick you up then. Ok baby, I will see you later then. Ok, bye honey. Click! Tonya hangs up the phone then leans back in her huge office chair with a big grin on her face.

Ring-Ring-Ring. Hello! Hey sis! What's up Tonya! Girl, Tim sent me a dozen red roses today! What, go ahead now! What are you doing tonight around 8 o'clock? Not a damn thing, what's up? Tim invited me out for sushi; can you watch the kids for me? Sure; I got you; you want me to pick them up too? Please! Ok, I got you; go have some fun. Alright sis, I will see you later tonight. Ok, bye girl. Simone hangs of the phone and walks in to the living room. Ding-Dong. The doorbell rings. She makes her way over to the door to see who it was; she pulls the curtain back and seen that it was the mail man.

Simone opens the door. Hey, how are you today Ma'am? I'm good; how can I help you? I have a certified letter here from the state of New York for Mrs. Simone Clarke. I'm Mrs. Clarke! Ok, just sign right here for me Ma'am. The mail man hands her a pen to sign for the letter. Alright, have a good day Mrs. Clarke. Thanks; you do the same. She closes the door as he continued on his route.

She makes her way in to the kitchen and takes a seat at the table then opens the envelope to see what was inside. The letter read as follows. "Dear Mrs. Clarke the state of New York has been working with the U.S Army to recover back child support for your two dependents that you share with Mr. Jason Clarke.

It has come to our attention that you are no longer a resident at housing unit 576 on Ft. Drum, N.Y. Army base. We have contacted SSG. Clarke and he stated that the two of you are separated and plan on getting a divorce.

Because of your current situation we find that it's only right that we award you alimony along with the back child support that your husband failed to pay. We have since deducted the benefit dependent amounts we awarded to your former spouse from his paychecks and will be forwarding you a check, twice a month to cover housing, daycare and cost of living. You will receive your checks on the 1st and 15th of every month.

Please find enclosed a back pay check in the amount of $15,795.98. We are sorry for any hardships that we have caused for our delinquency in responding to your claim and hope that this will take care of your situation. Thanks for your time. Major: John Cunningham; Finance Division."

Simone stands up in the kitchen chair then jumps on the table. Holy shit! Woooo-Hoooo! Yes! Yes! Thank you Jesus! She gets down from the table; runs in the living room to turn on the radio as loud as it would go. "Hey what's up New York, This is your girl Angie, come check me out today over at Prospect park for the annual free concert. Right now let's keep it going with some of that Big Daddy Kane. "Here I am… R-A-W terrorist" "Here to bring trouble to phoney emcees" "I move on and seize, just conquer'. Simone's in the middle of the living room, dancing a happy dance and looking at her-self in the mirror as she attempts to do the dances she seen in Kane's video.

Ding-Dong. The doorbell rings but she can't hear it over the loud music. Ding-Dong. Knock-Knock-Knock! Simone! Open the door girl! She pauses for a minute then turns down the radio. Knock-Knock-Knock! Who is it! Lisa child! Oh, I'm coming! She opens the door. Hey girl! What's up bitch, you having a party all by yourself! Ha-ha-ha. Hell yeah!

Damn, give me some of what you're drinking; it got you open like that! Bitch I aint drinking shit; here; read this. She hands Lisa the letter. I'm going to celebrate girl! Oh shit; you lucky bitch! I would be happy too! Go ahead now! Yeah girl, I'm good! Yep, go ahead and let a bitch get a thousand? Simone stops dancing and looks at Lisa. See just like a nigga; hell no girl.

Come on; I will pay you back! Ha-ha-ha. You good girl; you know I got you!

Thank you child; now I can get Scott's ass out of jail! What! When did that happen? Last night child, this fool was at the bar drunk as hell as usual and walked out without paying his tab; cursed the owner out and the police officer. They put his butt in the drunk tank and told him if no one bailed him out in 48 hours he had to do 30 days. Damn that's messed up!

Don't feel sorry girl; he did that shit to his-self. I'll get him tomorrow with that money you're going to loan me, his ass can sit there for now. Let's celebrate!

Hold on; let me get my shoes, so you can take me to the bank. Ok. Lisa gets off the couch to wait for her by the door. Simone slips on her shoes and head out to the car with Lisa. Ring-Ring-Ring. Simone's cell phone starts to ring. She took a seat on the passenger's side of the Volvo. Hello! Hey sexy! Heeeey Cap! What you getting in to over on Long Island? Well I'm on the way to the bank right now to cash my $15,000.00 check nigga!

Yeah whatever! I'm serious baby! The Army sent my back pay check today! Wow that's good baby; don't spend it all in one place. Wait! Why did the Army send you a check? Because I am a dependent remember; my ex-husband wasn't sending any child support or alimony. Nothing!

Nope, not a damn thing baby! Damn! Well I have to get back to work; I will speak with you later and don't spend all of that money in one place. Okay bye sugar! Jeron turns on the TV, grabs some chips from the counter and makes his way to the couch.

Knock-Knock-Knock. Who is it! It's Erin! It's open; come in baby! Erin was a 19 year old college student that went to N.Y.U.; she stood 5'2" with shoulder length blonde hair, nice size breast and a cheer leader's body. They met last year while she was a senior in

High School and came to visit her brother on base.

Erin walks in the door wearing a red fitted sweater and blue jeans with red knee high leather boots. Damn baby; you're looking sexy as a motherfucker in that sweater and jeans. Why are your nipples so hard baby; them things are poking through your sweater. Ha-ha-ha. You think that's something you should feel how wet my pussy is! Really! Yep! She makes her way over to the couch and takes a seat beside him.

I called your ass the other day too Jeron! I know baby; I had a lot going on; how's school going? It's ok, I just have to study my ass off. You must not have any classes today? I only had two, earlier today; I'm done until tomorrow. What's your major again? Mechanical Engineering! Really! Yep! Can we fuck; I'm horny as hake!

Your ass, always wanna fuck! Because! Because what? You got that good dick, that's why and it feels so good inside me! Erin takes off her boots then slouches back down on the couch, unzips her jeans, slides them off and sits them on the floor. She props her left leg up on the edge of the sofa. Damn girl that pussy clean; did you just shave? Yep! Look how wet it is. She takes her pointer and index finger of her right hand then spreads her vagina open. See look!

The juices flowed down the center of her pussy to the bottom, right above her asshole. Hmmm, that looks good too. Come on and fuck me; you know you want too. Cap slid up to the edge of the sofa and faced her then slowly stuck two fingers from his right hand in her wet womb. Ooooohh yeah! Ooooo yeah! Oooooh yeah. Come on and put in; please. Jeron removed his hand and stood up to take off his shorts. Yeah fuck me! Hurry up!

He reached down to get a condom from under the end couch pillow where he kept his stash. Noooooo. Come on; fuck me raw;

come on, put it in me. Erin grabbed a hold of his dick; stood up and turned around. Slide it in J; hit it from the back. Come on; I want you inside me.

Hurry up baby; I'm so horny; it's not gonna take long. Jeron stood there with a blank stare on his face trying to decide if he wanted to hit it raw dog. Shhhhhhh. What the fuck are you Girl!

Erin had slid back on his hard Johnson and started to move slowly back and forth. Damn, you wet as fuck! I told you; come on, give it to me; make it fast, I'm having lunch with my brother in a few. Cap grabbed her by the waist and stroked the pussy with a hard thrust in, then slowly out. Ohhhh yeah! Ohhhh yeah! Fuck me! You like that bitch! Yes! Yes! Fuck me! He thrust hard again then pulled out slow. Shit! Why you teasing me Jeron; fuck me! Uhhhhh!

He stroked her again and again, and again, and again and again. Yes, that's it! Damn, this is some wet pussy girl! Yesss! Yess! I'm

Cumming baby! Yes! Erin fell down face first on the couch. Oh shit! He ducked then fell to the floor. What the fuck is that! Her juices had squirted across his shoulder while she was Cumming. Wow! I told you I was horny baby. Ha-ha-ha. I see! Ha-ha-ha. They both laugh.

She gets up from the couch and head to the restroom to wash her-self off. Thank you so much Jeron; I needed that! Damn, I have ten minutes to meet my brother; can you hand me my jeans please. Sure; where are you guys having lunch? I don't know; he's taking me somewhere off base. Here you go baby. Thanks. She slips on her jeans and walk back over to the couch to put on her boots. Man you need to answer your phone when I be calling your ass too. Girl I have a company to run; you know I be busy and shit. Hmmmmm-Hmmmmm.

Muah! She kisses him on the cheek. I will talk to you later and thanks again for fucking me! Ha-ha-ha. You're welcome; it's not a problem; glad I could help. Ha-ha-ha.

Whatever; bye Jeron! Bye baby! He closes the door behind her and she makes her way up the barracks hallway.

Cap goes to the bathroom to start a hot shower; so he could wash up and return to work. The mirror fogged and walls started to sweat as he stepped in under his adjustable shower head and washed his face then rest of body. 5 minutes pass and Captain Briggs turned off the water and stepped out of the shower, dried off then put on his BDU's.

In a rush he made his way over to his bed to put on his jump boots. Jeron laced up his shoes, walked into the hallway, locked the door behind him and headed to his office. Hey Captain Briggs; LT called and said for you to give him a call regarding the cadet interviews. Ok Sgt; are they any other messages? No that's it.

Cap. Stood in the doorway of his office looking over some documents he picked up from his in box. He leaned back against the door molding then felt an itch on his upper right thigh; so he reached in his right pocket to scratch it through his Bdu's. Ok Sgt.; call LT back and have him schedule the cadet interviews for tomorrow; I have to finish up these reports today. Ok Cap! If anyone else calls tell them I'm busy and take a message.

Yes Sir! Jeron makes his way in his office and takes a seat behind the desk. Fuck! Why am I itching so damn much! He stood up; reached in his pants and started to scratch above his pubic hairs. It continued to get worse after he scratched.

The itching began to annoy him; so he unbuckled his belt then dropped his pants. After taking a closer look he saw that his pubic hairs all had a white substance at the root and seemed to be coming out of his skin. Damn, what the fuck is going on. He picked up the phone to call the medics office downstairs.

Ring-Ring-Ring. Hello Medics office. Yes this is Captain Briggs; is Warrant Officer Brown in? Yes sir; hold please. Hello this is Officer Brown! Hey Brown this is Briggs! Hey man what's going on? Brother I think something is wrong with my pubic hairs and shit! What do you mean bruh? Dude they look white at the root and I'm itching like crazy! Ha-ha-ha. Man who have you been fucking with-in the last 24 hours?

I just laid this young chic not even two hours ago? Why; do you know what's wrong? I think so! Where are you right now? In my office! Ok, do you have one of those military issued desk calendars? Yes! OK, I want you to drop your pants and lean over that calendar then rub your hand through your pubic hairs. Ok hold on; I'll put you on speaker phone. Jeron puts the officer on speaker phone then leans over the desk and brush through his hairs. What the fuck! He noticed little small critters falling on the white paper. Man, what the hell is this shit! Tell me what you see Cap! Little bugs man! Pick one up and tell me what it looks like. Ok.

He places one of his business cards on the calendar and scoops one up. I have one! What does it look like? He puts it up closer so he could see. Brown, this looks like a crab bruh!

Yeah I was afraid of that! Someone gave you crabs; that's why your pubic hairs look white at the root, they were pulling them out, which caused you to itch. Man I'm gone beat that white bitch ass! You need to let her know so she can get it taken care of; we don't want anyone else to get infected.

Fuck her bruh; what about me? Come downstairs and I can give you some ointment to kill them off and cure you. Thanks man; I'm on the way! Ok Cap!

He hangs up the phone then calls Erin. Ring-Ring-Ring. Hi you've reached Erin; sorry I missed your call, please leave a message. Hey, you need to call me ASAP! Click!

Jeron buttons his pants, tightens his belt then head downstairs to see the medic. Hey Sgt; I will be back in a few! Ok Sir! Jeron left the office with an angry expression on his face and mumbling under his breath. I'm gone whip that white whores ass; wait until I see that bitch. I hope that slut aint got shit else; Fuck! My stupid ass hit it raw too. He shakes his head as he enters the stairwell to go downstairs to the first floor.

Jeron exits the stairwell and makes a left into the hallway; two doors down from the stairs was the medic's office sitting at the end of the hall. Captain approached the window. Hello Sir; how can I help you?

Hi; I need to see Officer Brown. Ok; one minute sir. The receptionist picks up the phone to page the officer. Officer Brown; Captain Briggs is here to see you! Ok; send him in! Yes sir! You can go in Captain. Thanks! He walks down to the end of the counter and enters the office door. Hey man come in, have a seat!

Doc; you got to help me brother; this bitch got me all fucked up! Calm down Cap; I will take care of it. Good; how long do I have to wait before I can have sex again? To be safe I would wait at least ten days, two weeks if possible. Damn, that long! Yep!

Doc reaches in his cabinet and pulls out a bottle of shampoo, cream and a razor. Alright Cap; shampoo your private area with this then take this razor and shave all your pubic hairs off about 4 hours afterwards. Once that's done apply this cream to your private area. Make sure you put the razor in a separate bag when you're done and throw it away. Damn, my shit is going to be bald! Hey that's what happen when you're not careful; make sure you tell her to get treated too. Ok Doc; thanks a lot man. You're welcome Cap!

Captain Briggs collects his medicine then leaves the medics office and heads back to his place to handle his situation.

5, The sum of all things.

It's the middle of May and the weather is fitting for the family cookout that Simone and Tonya are having; to welcome their parent's home.

The grass is freshly cut and hedges trimmed around the Long Island home, the sun had just set around 6pm, several cars jammed the driveway and street curb. Half a dozen kids are running in between the cars in the driveway and over the front lawn, while playing tag. A red brick walkway led to the back yard where the adults were grilling the food; drinking, playing cards and dancing. Sounds of laughter filled the air as they all enjoyed this joyous occasion. Sitting over on the back step was this grey haired, dark skinned gentleman wearing a royal blue Nike sweat suit and white sneakers.

Two little girls sat on the steps beside him and watched as he lit his caramel colored tobacco pipe and placed it to his lips. What are you doing pa pa? Smoking my pipe honey! It stinks pa pa! Yeah, it stinks pa pa! The two girls get up from the steps and run around to the front lawn to play with the other kids.

Dad! Yes Simone, what is it? How did you want your steak? Medium well baby! Did you find a man while we were gone girl? Dad! What! I'm serious! Well did you? Yeah I did! Well thank God for that; where is he? Ha-ha-ha. His name is Jeron and he will be here shortly. Good; what does this fella do for a living? He's a Captain over at West Point! You got yourself an officer baby girl, good for you. I can't wait to meet him; where's Craig?

Oh I better let Tonya tell you about that one! Damn, what done happen now? Simone walks off and heads to the grill while calling her sister. Tonya! Tonya! What girl! Dad wants you? Ok I'm coming! She picks up her glass of crown from the table and heads over to her father. What's up pops! Where is that husband of yours? Man I kicked him out for cheating on me; he slept with my employee dad, at my office on top of that. Wow, I don't know what this world is coming to; nobody is faithful anymore.

I hope you really plan on divorcing that fool this time baby. Don't worry dad; this time he took it too far. Ok I hear you; come here and let daddy give you a hug. Tonya walks up to her father, he stands up off the steps and gives her a great big loving hug. Muah! I love you baby girl, everything will work itself out, don't you worry. I know dad, I know, thank you. Where's Mom at anyway, she should have been downstairs by now.

Man that woman was messing with her feet last time I seen her. There's no telling what she's doing now baby! Hey Pops! Well; I'll be damn! Hey Lisa! Hey Scott, what the hell happen to your arm fella?

Pops it's nothing, me and Lisa just had a fight, that's all. Damn she still whipping that ass huh, I guess you like getting beat on by your woman, huh Scott! Ha-ha-ha. That's some crazy love yall got Lisa! Pops, he keeps messing up, so I keep beating that ass! Ha-ha-ha. I guess!

Come on Scott, walk over here with me and let's get a beer. Pops get up from the steps and stand beside Scott; he seemed like a giant as his 6'5" frame towered over him. They walked over to the picnic table that sat under the oak tree where the beer cooler was.

The back door opened and out walked a short stubby, grey haired woman, wearing sandals and a white linen dress. In her hand she held a medium sized boom box which she placed on the porch before turning it on. Ok people let's get this party started, it aint a party without no music. Ok Mom, get it started baby! Simone yelled out.

Moms turned the boom box on and stuck a cassette in the tape player. Family Reunion by The O Jays was playing. "It's so nice to see" "All the folks you love together" "Sittin and talkin bout" "All the things that's been going down".

Yeah Mom, that's it right there baby! Tonya shouts. Sing it Momma! "Family Reunion (got to have)" "A family Reunion" "Family Reunion".Ohhhhh yeah, come on yall! All the relatives stood up and started to dance. Tonya was shaking her butt as she flipped the burgers on the grill. Mommy! Mommy! What Twin? Daddy is here!

Tonya's son ran in the back yard to tell her the news. Quit playing son. He is mommy, he is! Tonya puts the spatula on the table beside the grill and walks around to the front yard to see for herself. Hey sis, where you going? Girl, twin said his dad is up front! What! Hold on, I'm coming with you! Simone ran up front with her sister. Craig and Sonya were walking up the driveway when the sisters made their way up front.

What the fuck! Nigga I know you didn't bring that trifling bitch to my mother's house! Calm down Tonya, calm down.

Don't tell me to calm down nigga; take that hoe away from here before she catches a bullet! Wait Tonya, I'm sorry! Shut up Sonya, don't say shit to me bitch. Craig, get the hell out of here or there's going to be trouble. Ok, ok I'm going! Come on Sonya; let's go. He takes Sonya by the hand and heads back to the car. Damn, can you believe the nerves of that fool Simone?

Girl that boy got issues, come on let's get back to the party. Beep-Beep-Beep. Who the hake is that blowing at us? Oh girl, that's Tim and Jeron! The two gentlemen pulled up in a white wrangler jeep and parked by the curb in front of the neighbor's house. The sisters walked to the end of the driveway to meet them. Hey baby! Simone reaches out to hug Jeron. Hi handsome! Muah! Tonya kisses Tim on the cheek and they escort the soldiers to the back yard. Hmmmm. It smells good out here, what you guys grilling? You like that huh Jeron, we got some burgers, chicken, ribs, corn and some hot links.

Damn, you guys are throwing down over here huh! Yep! Come on back and get a plate! They make their way to the back to join the others. Tim and J had just left drill and came straight over still dressed in their Battle Dress Uniforms. Simone stopped in the center of the backyard and introduced the guys. Hey everybody this is Jeron and Tim, guys this is everybody! Hey everybody! Hey! Everyone shouted.

Hey sis, take them over to meet pops I'm going to finish up on the grill. Ok Tonya; hurry up too, something is burning. Ha-ha-ha. Shut up girl, that's going to be your piece! Yeah whatever! Ha-ha-ha. Come on fellas! The soldiers follow her over to the picnic table under the tree where pop is sitting. Dad this is Jeron and Tim; fellas this is my dad. Hi sir!

Hello gentlemen; sit down and have a beer; this guy over here is Scott. Hi Scott! Hi fellas! They join the guys at the table and grab a cold beer from the cooler. Pops takes off his jacket and leans forward over the table then places his forearms down in front of him. So how long have you guys been in the Army? We came in 5 years ago sir; did you ever serve? Have I! Ha-ha-ha.

He laughs then rolls up the right sleeve of his T-shirt to reveal a tattoo. Wow ok! Jeron spoke out. Fort Hood huh, Cavalry! Yes sir; I retired as a Major about 15 years ago. I got this here tatt when I was just a LT over in Thailand; during Cobra Gold.

Well it's nice to meet you Major! Nice to meet you gentlemen; what say your rank? I'm a Captain Sir and my friend here is a 1st LT. Good; I'm hungry are you guys hungry? Yes sir! Hey baby girl how long before the food is ready? 5 minutes dad! Ok baby!

Moms; walks off the back porch and makes her way over to the picnic table. Oh boy;

here comes the misses; Scott; grab her a cold one out of the cooler will you champ? Sure! He reaches in and gets a cold can of beer. Hello gentlemen! Hi Ma'am! Sweetie, fill this cup up for me please. She hands pops a blue solo cup.

Scott hands him the beer. Sweetie did you tell these soldiers that both our daughters are still married! Honey please; I'm sure the girls told them and that's not our business anyway. Here take your beer baby and go join the others; I love you. Yeah, yeah ok, don't be trying to run me off either. Ha-ha-ha. He laughs as she walks away. I love that woman but she can be a handful sometimes.

Ok everyone the food is ready; kids go wash your hands! Moms, Simone and Lisa gather behind the table and prepare to serve the food.

Jeron takes a sip of beer and puts it back on the table. Say pops; did you enjoy your tour in the service? What! Did I! Man let me tell you about this time I went to Thailand; boy it's some beautiful ladies over there. Pops stop playing; aint' no fine girls in Thailand!

See here young blood that's where you're wrong; you need to take a trip over there before you get out of the service; see for yourself. Hey Cap; we got Cobra Gold coming up in a few weeks; that's in Thailand; in Karat I believe. Yep that's where we went years ago; stayed over on Camp Friendship.

We'll we might have to join the troops this time and see what Thailand has to offer. Go ahead soldier, take the trip, I promise you won't regret it. Alright fellas! Stop trading war stories and come eat. Ok! Ok Momma we're coming! I see who wears the pants in this family Pops!

Only when I let her young blood! Only when I let her! The guys stand up and make their way over to the table. The food all looked and smelled delicious sitting on the table as they approached. Juicy ears of corn, BBQ pork ribs, Hamburgers, Grilled chicken legs, hot links and wings along with fresh salad and pasta made up the menu.

Tim stood in line behind the last kid and waited for his plate to be filled by the ladies. Well what are you having Tim? Oh give me some of everything Ma'am! Ok coming right up! Moms grabbed a paper plate from the end of the table and placed two spoons of pasta salad on his plate along with some ribs and passed it down to Simone.

Pops came up next. Honey did you take your blood pressure pills today? Yeah Momma! Ok because you're not getting any of these ribs if you didn't! Woman would you please fix my plate so I can eat, I'm starving over here.

She smiles then continues to fix her husband a plate. The others join the line and prepare to receive their meals. Joyful laughter filled the air as the kids sat at the table enjoying each other only as they could. Pops, Jeron, Tim and Scott made their way back over to the picnic table where they were previously sitting.

Lisa, Tonya, Simone and Mom finish up with the serving then fix themselves a plate. Hey Mom can you put me two ribs on here for me? Sure baby, here you go. She places some ribs on Simone's plate along with some salad. Here you go sweetie, I put some veggies on there for you too.

Thanks Momma! Hmmm –Hmmm. Mom I don't want any salad, so don't put any on mine. Tonya you need to eat some salad, you can't just eat meat! Mom; no salad! Ok-Ok-Ok! She puts one rib on the plate and proceeds to pass it down. Mom! What! Stop playing!

I'm not playing, If you want more ribs, you need to get some salad! Uhhhh! Ok only a little bit! Alright that's my girl! Mom adds two more ribs along with a serving of salad.

Here you are darling! Thank you Mom! You're welcome! Lisa did you want any? Yes

Ma'am! She fixed another plate of salad and ribs for Lisa. Thank you Ma'am! You're welcome!

The ladies continued to fixed their plates and found a seat at the table adjacent to the patio stairs. Lisa picked up her purse from the chair, reached in and grabbed a bottle of Hennessy.

Hey Tonya; pour me a cup of that coke will you? Sure girl! Only half a cup though baby. Lisa I aint stupid, I hope you got enough for me too. Bitch I got a half a gallon, about to crack it now. You want some too Simone? Yep! Pour it up!

Soooo Sis; what's up with some of that loot you got girl? Nothing, in the damn bank! When you going shopping? Tomorrow! Ha-ha-ha! Bitch you crazy! Well it's the truth. I know it is; that's why I laughed at your crazy ass. No I'm just kidding; I'm going to check out these Condo's around the block.

Oh ok; that's what's up. Shit; I don't know why you're moving, mom and dad leaving again in a few weeks to go to New Orleans, to stay with Aunt Jackie for the summer anyway.

I want to check them out and see if I could get one if I need too. Girl your credit straight, it want be a problem. Yeah you may be right but I'm going anyway.

Lisa pours some Hennessy in the three cups that sat on the table. Stop fussing bitches and drink up! Shut up Lisa. I'm just saying Tonya; it aint no big deal. She looks over at both the sisters and with two hands, slides their cups over in front of them. Now drink up! Ha-ha-ha. You a nut!

The sun had set and the sky turned dark as the street lights and motion lights surrounded the house illuminated. Once full plates, were now empty, the kids went inside, mom and pops joined them as Scott, Tim and Jeron made their way over to the table with the ladies.

Lisa removed the half gallon of Henn from her purse and placed it in the center of the table. Scott took a fifth of E&J from his pocket and sat it down as well. Damn you two came prepared huh! Tim as long as these two are at the party we're in good hands baby! Ha-ha-ha! Shut up Tonya!

Scott, you know it's true! Damn right baby, tell em, we always got drinks on deck. Muah! Lisa leans over and kisses her husband on the lips. Ok you two, let me get some of that Henndog. Hey; you got to pour your own troubles Jeron; here, help yourself. She hands him the bottle.

Thanks Lisa! Yep, don't mention it! A few minutes as well as a couple of rounds had passed. The bottles were now empty and their spirits full of liquid courage. So tell me fellas, you and, and, and you the two soldiers, soldiers. Scott had stood to his feet and pointed at the officers as he staggered a little and begun to stutter his words.

Yeah, what is it Scott? Hey, Hey, Hey, just hold, hold on a minute, I'm the one answering the questions, questions!

Dammit, dammit! Baby, sit your drunk ass down! Lisa, don't, don't tell me to sit down woman, woman.

Ha-ha-ha! Everyone at the table laughed at him as he stood there making a fool of himself. See this is the kind of shit I have to deal with; drunk ass husband; damn fool can't handle his liquor! Lisa yelled out loud. Scott sit down or I'm gonna knock your ass out!

Hey Bitch, shut up! Whoa! Hold on brother; that's not called for. Fuck you Tim! I can talk to my wife anyway I want! Man, just have a seat and calm down. He looks at Tim, wobbles a little then points his finger at him.

You shut the fuck up and mind your business soldier boy, that's, that's, that's what you do na-na-nigga! SMACK! Scott falls back over the chair and hits the ground. Tim is standing there over him and preparing to smack him again. Whoa bro!

That's enough, have a seat! Jeron ran over to stop him from smacking Scott again.

Tim looks over at Cap then reaches down to help Scott up. I'm sorry man but your ass was getting out of hand. Scott gets up to his feet, rubs the right side of his face with his free hand, tucks his shirt back in his jeans and walks off. Hey baby wait, wait! Lisa yells then gets up from the table and runs after him.

Wow, Tim I can't believe you just smacked my friends husband. My bad Tonya but that fool was getting out of line. Yeah he's always like that when he drinks. Then that nigga don't need to drink, if it's like that. Simone is just sitting there shaking her head at the entire debacle.

Tonya, Tim, Jeron and Simone all get up from the table then picks up the empty liquor bottles and cups and put them in the trash. Tonya walks up the back steps and opens the door to the house. Come on guys there's some fresh apple pie in the oven and some vanilla ice cream in the deep freezer. Hell yeah! The fellas yelled out as they followed them inside and joined the sisters for a late dessert.

6, Family Matters.

It's a sunny Monday afternoon over at West Coast Image, Tonya, Craig and their divorce Attorneys are all sitting in the conference room. Mrs. Sinclair; Tonya's Attorney has the floor and starts to discuss the decree. Ok Craig; my client wants full custody of the kids and you can make arrangements to see them on the weekend and holidays.

You may also pick them up from school and attend any events involving them as far as sports and any extra-curricular activities. As far as your night club; my client wants you to buy her out; in which case you will get her 40% for $45,000.00.

She doesn't care to place you on child support and will not be asking for any alimony if you agree to the buy-out. If however you disagree with the buy-out we will proceed with a request for child support as well as alimony.

We are prepared to sign today to make the divorce final; the other stipulations we can sign also, if you agree to the above terms. Do you understand the terms as I've read them sir? Hold on Mrs. Sinclair let me speak with my client first before we give you an answer. Sure Mr. Wallace, take your time.

Craig and Mr. Wallace get up from the table and walk over to the far corner by the large picture window over-looking the city. So do you agree with all the terms Craig? Shit, I don't know man; what do you think? Well if you want to get this mess behind you and get on with your life, I would take the offer.

Hmmm, if I buy her out, I want be on any child support or alimony; that does sound tempting. Yeah, I think you should accept. You can sign the papers today and put this divorce behind you and you will own %100 of your club to boot.

He looks his attorney in the eyes; shakes his hand and they proceed to the table. Well; what will it be Mr. Wallace? Where do we sign Mrs. Sinclair? She smiles, reaches in her briefcase and hands Craig the papers. Here you are sir. Tonya leans back in her seat, folds her arms and looks at Craig with a disgusting look as he signs.

He finished completing the papers and slides them back over to Mrs. Sinclair so Tonya could sign. Wait a minute; I aint signing that until I get my check! Craig sits there shaking his head then reaches in his suit jacket to get his check book.

Yeah that's right; give me my money, today! He smirks and slams the check book on the table, opens it and writes the check and signs it. Thank you! She snatches it from his hands, sticks it in her bra then proceeds to sign the divorce decree. Tonya then stands up and looks at everyone in the room. Well, I would like to thank you guys for making this an easy process and Craig this check better not bounce or I'm gonna put two slugs in your black ass!

Yeah whatever woman, hope you enjoy your new life; with your crazy ass. Don't worry, I will! The attorney's shakes hands then exit the room behind Craig, and Tonya follows them out.

Over on Long island; Simone's, going through her own dilemma. She's sitting on the living room couch in a long T-shirt and socks chatting on the phone with Jeron. So when am I going to see you again baby? We can meet up tomorrow if you want; I am only working a half day too. Really! Yes, really Simone.

Knock-Knock-Knock. Some ones knocking softly at his door; Jeron rises up from the couch holding the cordless phone to his right ear. He continues talking to Simone as he goes to answer it. I can't wait to see you baby; I missed you. I miss you too! Stop lying Jeron; you're just saying that because I said it. Ha-ha! No girl, I'm serious.

As he approached the door the soft tapping became louder. Jeron unlocks it, opens it and there she was. He snatches his visitor by her collar with his free hand and pulls her inside. She shouts. What the fuck J! What was that honey? Do you have company? No baby that was one of the soldiers walking down the hallway.

Cap looks at his visitor and with his eyes, motions her to sit down on the couch. She snatches away from him then sits down. He began to pace back and forth between the TV and the couch while talking to Simone on the phone. What's wrong babe, you seem distracted. Nothing, I'm good baby; what were you saying?

Oh, I wanted to know what time was I going to see you tomorrow? Sometime around two o'clock I'm thinking. Good, I can't wait! The visitor sat there impatiently waiting for him to end his telephone conversation.

Cap stopped pacing then leaned back on the arm of the couch with the phone to his ear. The visitor reached down and removed her shoes, pulled her long blonde hair back and tied it up.

She slid down to the end of the couch where he was, so that she would be right behind him as he continued talking on the phone. So what are you wearing baby? Well I'm sitting here on the couch in only a T-shirt and socks; wishing you was here with me.

Oh yeah, is that right. Yes! So what will we be doing if I was there with you? Ummmm. I would unzip your pants, massage your dick then suck it until you can't cum anymore. Damn baby, that sounds good, what else would you do? He reached down with his free hand and started to rub on his Johnson as she continued talking to him.

I would remove my clothes so that I could play with myself while I was giving you head. Ummm. I like that! Yeah I thought you would Captain! Jeron continue to stand there leaning against the arm of the chair with his hand on his jock. While he was standing there with his eyes closed and being mesmerized by Simone's every word something was happening.

All of sudden every word she spoke became vivid like she was really there. He felt her pull his penis out then she placed those soft wet lips around his hard dick. Damn, that feels good baby, keep going don't stop! Yeah you like that huh? Hell yeah; I can almost feel you sucking on me.

Yeah, do it slow baby, yes just like that. Ahhh, you feel so good. As he closed his eyes his natural reaction was to reach down and grab her hair. Forgetting that she was on the other side of the call he reached down anyway. What the fuck! Baby! Baby! What's wrong!

Erin, get your ass up! Baby! Baby! Simone was calling him to see what was going on. Jeron had dropped the phone after being shocked. Erin kept on blowing him as he relaxed and fell back against the arm of the couch. Shit, that feels so damn good. She looked up at him with her blue eyes and her mouth full of penis.

The dial tone had sounded from the phone after Simone hung up. Cap grabbed Erin by the hair and guided her head as she continued to perform what he felt like the best oral sex he ever had. His ass cheeks clinched, toes curled and his hands squeezed her head a little tighter as he released in her mouth.

Ding-Dong! Damn, who is that! Simone shouted as she tried to call Cap back. Ding-Dong! She placed the phone on the hook then proceeded to answer her door. Who is it! It's me honey! Me who! She looked through the peep hole. Hell nah! She went to the desk that her father kept in the front room and got the loaded 22 caliber pistol from the bottom left drawer.

Simone then ran back to the door and opened it. Nigga you done bumped your motherfucking head! What are you doing here? I came to see the kids, baby. Ha-ha-ha. You are too funny; all this time and you want to see the kids now; after Uncle Sam cut your check short! You aint shit nigga!

Well they're not here anyway. Where are they? None of your business, you best be going. I have company coming over. Come on Mone; stop tripping! Boy you tripping, coming over here now after all this time. Girl I was busy; it aint even like that. Yeah whatever, stop lying.

I'm not lying! Whatever, it's time for you to go. Ok but when can I see the kids? Call me tomorrow and I will let you know. Ok thanks! Yeah bye! He walks away as she slams the door behind him.

Meanwhile downtown at the Long Island City probation office; Lisa and Scott are there speaking with his P.O. Well Scott it looks like you really done it this time sir. I know Mr. Silas, that damn alcohol just brings the worse out of me.

Yep, you're right about that! So this is the deal, we're putting you on some no drinking pills. What's that sir? Ma'am, it's a pill he has to take once a day and if he drinks any alcohol while he's on them he will throw it back up. Throw it back up! You mean vomit! Yes Ma'am!

Damn! Hold on Scott, there's more. We also have you schedule to come in once a week to do a drug and alcohol test. If you test positive, you will be incarcerated for 3-6 months.

Shit! Really! Yes Sir. Scott stands up and starts to pace back and forth in front of Mr. Silas's desk. Sit down honey, this is good for you. Do you guys understand everything as I have explained it to you? Yes Sir, we heard you loud and clear.

Great, now I just need both you guys to sign and date here, while I go get the pills. He hands them a pen then gets up and leaves his office. Baby you better not fuck this up or you're going to jail! I'm serious Scott! Yeah, I want baby. You better not! They both sign the document and slide it to his side of the desk.

 Mr. Silas walks back in the office. Ok here you go Sir, take one a day and remember no drinking. Ok. He takes a seat at his desk and flips through his desk calendar. Hmmm. What days do you have off Scott? Sunday and Monday sir! Great, come see me every Monday at 2pm! Alright; I will see you next week. Good!

Mr. Silas stands up and shakes both Lisa and Scotts hand before they leave his office. Have a great evening guys and good luck Scott! Thanks! Lisa opens the door and they head home.

Ring-Ring-Ring. Hello thank you for calling Nassau County School, this is Melissa how may I help you? Hi Melissa this is Craig. Hi Craig, what's going on? I'm running a little behind today and it's my turn to pick up the kids, so I'm sending Sonya my fiancé to get them, is that ok? Sure I will let the VP know. Ok, thank you so much Melissa. No problem sir, have a good evening. Thanks, you too! Melissa hangs up the phone then dials another number.

Ring-Ring-Ring. WCI how may I help you? Can I speak with Tonya please? Sure may I ask who is calling? It's Melissa from Nassau County Schools. Ok hold on. Buzz-Buzz. Yes! Tonya there's a Melissa on line one for you from Nassau County Schools. Ok put her through.

Hey Melissa, what's up; is there something wrong? I'm just calling to let you that Craig called and said that he is sending his fiancé to pick up the kids today. What! His fiancé! Why isn't he doing it? He said he was running behind. Hmmm-mmm. Thank you girl! You're welcome Tonya! Alright, I will speak with you tomorrow. Ok bye!

Tonya hangs up the speaker phone then reclines back in her office chair. She pulls a bottle of Merlot from the wine shelf behind her desk and pops the bottle. Tonya was feeling some kind of way about the call she just received but really what could she do. They were divorced and he had his own life and apparently Sonya was going to be a part of it and her input didn't matter.

Buzz-Buzz. Yes what is it? There's a delivery here for you! What is it? Ahhhh! It's ahhhh. Just send them back here. Yes mam! The delivery guy walked in the office. Tonya is sitting behind her desk sipping on the glass of wine. Uhhmm-Uhhmmm! She cleared a throat after almost choking. Who's that for? She asked the delivery guy. He looked at the card. It says for my dear Tonya! Really! Yes Ma'am.

He walks closer to the desk and sits down the 3 dozen red roses and a box of cherry filled chocolates. Wow! Who is it from? He looks at the card once more. It says from Tim; Ma'am! Ha-ha-ha! Wow! She laughed out loud then continued smiling ear to ear.

The delivery guy cleared his throat. Umm-Umm. He moved closer to the desk.

There's one more thing Ma'am. What is it? He braces him-self and starts to sing to her. "Always and forever, each moment with you" "Is just like a dream to me that somehow came true". Tonya sat there in Aw as tears fell from her eyes while he sung Heatwaves; Always and forever. "And I know tomorrow will still be the same" "Cause we've got a life of love that want ever change and'…. Ok, Stop I can't take any more. Thank you, I can't stop crying now.

You're welcome Ma'am; enjoy the rest of your day. The delivery guy smiled at her then exited the office. She immediately picked up the phone to call Tim. Ring-Ring.

Hello! Hey you! Hi baby, I take it you got your surprise. Yessssss! Thank you baby! You're welcome. You made my day with that move; I love your crazy ass. I love you too baby. Awwwww. Are you coming over later so I can see you? Yes Ma'am. Good, I will see you then babe, get back to work and thank you soooo much. Ok babe, see you later.

7, The Storm.

It's another warm summer evening on Long Island; Lisa and Scott are sitting on their front porch. The neighborhood kids were playing out front under the street lights as the temperature soared towards 95%.

Scott while sitting on the top step opened a pack of cigarettes and pulled one out for him and another for his wife. Here you go baby, where's the lighter? Thanks honey, its right here. Lisa picked up the lighter from the window seal.

  She lit his cigarette then her own. With his cigarette in the corner of his mouth he leaned back against the porch and stretched his legs down the steps. Well I'll be damn, aint this some shit! What the hell! The couple shouted as the entire block went dark; street lights as well as every ones power were now out.

The kids laughed and ran inside to get some empty jelly jars and quarter water bottles from their homes. Then they gathered in the grassy area in between their houses and proceeded to chase the light bugs that lit up the dark night. Every other second you could see orange glows of light sparkle all around the house. Damn this shit happens every summer; we pay too much damn taxes for this! Lisa is in a rage and leaves the front porch to go inside.

Scott turns around to see if she went inside or was just standing there. He then reached in his back pocket and pulled out a fifth of E&J, took two swigs and stuck it back in his back pocket. Hey honey! Yes baby! I'm fixing a glass of tea, did you want some? Sure!

Lisa comes back outside with two glasses of tea. Here you are baby. Thanks! Scott takes the glass and drinks a few swallows. Uhhmm-Uhhmm. What's wrong baby; is it too sweet? Uhhmm-Uhhmm. He rises up from the steps, hand over his mouth. Baby!

Uhhmm-Uhhmm. Tears begin to fill his eyes as he continues to choke and cough.

She runs down the steps to his aid. Scott's eyes had become blood-shot. Lisa started to worry then ran inside to get the car keys.

Scott fell to his knees coughing and clinching his stomach. His wife ran back outside with the keys, picked him up and walked him to the front seat of the car. Baby! Baby lean back so I can put your seat belt on. Uhhmm-Uhhhmm. He continued to clear his throat and cough relentlessly. Nooo. Uhhmmm-Uhhhmmm. Where we going! Uhmm-Uhhm. The emergency room baby!

He shook his head, continued to cough and just leaned against the car window. Lisa accelerated up the street with her hazard lights on, running several red lights and stop signs until she reached the hospital. Seven minutes later they arrived. She jumped out, car still running and ran around to the passenger's side to get her husband out.

Two nurse's standing out front on what look like their smoke break, noticed Lisa trying to get Scott out of the car. They put out their cigarettes and ran over to help. Excuse me Ma'am! Here, lift him up, we can walk him in. What's the problem, did he swallow something? I don't know Ma'am, last I remember he was drinking some ice tea then just started choking and coughing relentlessly.

Ok, let's get him to the ER. They walk Scott inside and lay him on a vacant bed that sat by the entrance. Scott's eyes were now bloodshot red and tears ran down the side of his face as he clinched his stomach. Ma'am is he on any kind of medication? Ahhh. Yes, his probation officer put him on some non-drinking pills a few weeks ago.

Non-drinking pills Ma'am! Yes! Ok, did he have any alcohol today? No Ma'am! Are you sure Ma'am? Yes! Ok, wait here while we go check him out, we will let you know something as soon as we can.

Lisa took a seat in the waiting area amongst the others. Both her legs were shaking uncontrollably as she waited impatiently for an update.

She started to look around the room at the other patrons who also had loved ones in the ER. Oh fuck! Dammit! She shouted. Lisa stood up and ran outside to the emergency entrance to park her car that she left running out front.

Mrs. Pettigrew! Mrs. Lisa Pettigrew! The nurse called for her. Excuse me; is there a Mrs. Pettigrew here? Lisa had just come through the emergency door and spotted the nurse. Excuse me Ma'am; is there any word on my husband yet? Are you Mrs. Pettigrew Ma'am? Yes I am! What's your husband's probation officers name, we need to call him to see what type of pills he gave him. Oh, it's Mr. Silas. Thank you Ma'am, your husband will be fine, we're pumping his stomach now.

You will be able to see him in a few. Thank God! Thank you so much Ma'am. You're welcome, have a seat and I will come get you when he's ready. Ok, thanks again! No problem, just doing my job Mrs. Pettigrew. The nurse walked away and headed over to the check in desk to use the phone.

Ring-Ring. Hello Nassau County Probation office; how may I help you? Yes this is Nurse Riley over at Nassau County ER; can I speak with Mr. Silas please? Sure; hold one moment. Thanks! Hello this is Mr. Silas. Hi Mr. Silas, sorry to call you so late; this is Nurse Riley over at Nassau ER. Yes, how can I help you?

Well we have a Mr. Scott Pettigrew here that says you gave him some non-drinking pills. Yes, that is correct; he received them a few weeks ago. Well apparently, he was drinking and the chemicals mixed with the alcohol and he is in our care now. Really! Yes sir! Thank you for calling Nurse Riley. I must advise you that an officer will be taking him in custody because he violated his probation. I will call the sheriff and have the officer on duty at the hospital detain him. Ok, I understand sir.

Thank you for calling I am on the way. No problem and you're welcome. Did you want me to tell his wife? Sure, you can have her call me if she wants but I will be there in 5 minutes. Nah, I'll let you tell her when you get here. Ha-ha-ha. Ok!

Lisa had calm down after hearing the good news. The excitement had made her thirsty and a bit hungry; she reached in her purse to get a few dollars. In the corner of the hallway sat two vending machines, one with drinks and other with snacks. She approached the snack machine and purchased a bag of popcorn then a coke from the other machine.

Mrs. Pettigrew! She turned around to see who was calling her. Hi Mr. Silas, what are you doing here? Well it's not good news I'm afraid. What is it! I have to take Scott with me for violating his probation! Why! What did he do? He was drinking alcohol, the doctor found it in his stomach, that's why he got sick. That motherfucker!

Well I'm taking him in now; did you want to see him before we lock him up? God help that fool! Yes! Mr. Silas walks over to the check in desk. Excuse me where's Mr. Pettigrew's room? Two doors down the hall sir, right there where that officer is standing. He and Lisa proceed down the hallway.

Lisa walks in the room in a rage. Fool, why in the hell did you drink! I'm sorry baby but I couldn't take it. Yeah whatever, give me your wallet and the money out of your pockets, you aint gone need it where you going. Damn fool. Mr. Silas walks over to the bed and stands beside Scott. Officer can you handcuff this gentleman please!

The officer walks over, lifts him to his feet and put on the cuffs. How long will he be locked up Mr. Silas? Three to six months Ma'am, depend on what the judge says.

Damn, you should be a shame of yourself Scott. She shakes her head as Mr. Silas, Scott and the officer head outside to the patrol car. Baby I'm sorry, please forgive me. Yeah whatever; don't drop the soap, call me when you get out, I'll send a cab to pick your stupid ass up.

As they walk out the emergency exit towards the car, Lisa went the opposite direction towards the parking lot. Sirens ring load as two ambulance pull up to the emergency entrance. In a rage she jumped in her car and slammed the door and took off. The tail lights from her car faded in the darkness as she headed towards the express way.

Heat from the passing car engines created an uncomfortable atmosphere along the city street curb. It made the 95% weather feel like, 115% against Craig's back. He sweated from head to toe while standing out front directing the sign crew as they placed a new sign above the club.

After the divorce he and Sonya decided to change the name of the club and do a re-launch. Alright Billy, lift it up on the right side just a little. Billy pulls the edge of the sign up from the top. How about now Craig? Yep that's it, screw it in and lock it down buddy!

I'm going inside to turn it on and see how it looks. Billy tightens the sign and climbs down from the ladder. He stood on the sidewalk in front of the club, looking up and waiting to see it lit. Craig comes back out to see how it looks. Hell yeah, player! Yeah that's nice boss.

Eight huge capital letters, silver faced, trimmed in black formed together to spell PLATINUM. Yep, welcome to Club Platinum baby the hottest club in New York City! Craig shouted as he stood there holding his nuts with one hand and sipping a beer with the other.

Good job Billy, how much do I owe you my man? Ahh, just give me $2,500.00. Cool, I'll be right back; you want a beer or something? Nah I'm good, I got another job to do. Alright, I'll be right back. Craig went to his office to fetch the money from his safe. He entered the room, turned on the lights and headed over to the safe he kept behind a huge Malcolm X picture.

He removed the picture then turned the dial three clicks to the left, two the right then three back to the left. The safe opens and there sat three stacks of money. What the fuck! It's only 15 gees here; where's my other 5 gees?

Craig normally kept 20 gees in the safe to handle day to day operations. The only other person that has the combination was Sonya after he changed the first combination that he and his ex-wife shared. That, damn Sonya! The crazy bitch probably went shopping with her stupid ass, fucking women can't live with them, can't live without them. He pulled $2,500.00 from one of the stacks, locked the safe and replaced the picture.

Craig went back out front to give Billy his money. Here you go brother, I appreciate that, you did a good job. Thanks Boss, anytime! I will get at you later this week; let me get to this other job. Alright Billy; see you later man. He locks the door behind him as he leaves then walks back over to the bar to call Sonya.

Ring-Ring. Hello! Sonya! Hey Sugar. What you doing? Nothing; sitting at the kitchen table cutting some potatoes for dinner. What you up to? Billy just left here; we got the new sign today. Really, how does it look baby? Damn good! Cool! Anyway, I need to ask you something. What is it? Did you take any money from the safe? Oh yeah, I took $5,000.00 yesterday. What for baby?

I needed some new rims on my Vette. Ha-ha-ha. Girl you crazy, I didn't see any new rims on your car. I know, I had to order them first, I pick them up tomorrow. Well next time ask me for the money, we need to keep at least 20 gees at the club at all times. Ok sugar, I'm sorry. Yeah it's ok, I will be home in an hour; I'm going to stop by the gym first. Alright sugar, see you later.

Crowds of people gathered in the parking lot, adults stood in pairs as kids ran around playing. Simone, Tonya, Tim and Jeron stood on base in front of Head Quarters as the troops and officers loaded the bus that would take them to the air strip. The parking lot was filled with troops and dependents as they gathered to see their loved ones off and say their good by's.

Simone stood in front of Cap and looked into his eyes. I'm going to miss you baby, 45 days is a long time for me to go without seeing you. Hey, it's going to be alright baby, I will call you every chance I get. You promise! Yes I promise. Cap reached into his pants pocket to get his keys. Here do me a favor; take my jeep to get an oil change next week; please!

Sure baby, is there anything else you need me to do? No that's it, just behave yourself and don't get into any trouble. Leaning against the bus, holding each other tight, the two love birds; Tim and Tonya were in the middle of a long intimate kiss.

Bam! Bam! Cap smacked the side of the bus. Ok, come on love birds it's about time we head out. Tonya gave Tim one last hug and went over to join her sister as they watched the fellas board the bus. Many of them only wished their loved ones could join them for 45 days in Thailand.

All the soldiers boarded the bus; Tim and Cap were the last two to get on as they hugged their girlfriends one last time. Muah! I will call you when we get a chance baby. Yeah; me too baby! Simone and Tonya eyes began to tear up as they finally boarded. The driver closed the door and pulled off slowly as the soldier's wave to their loved ones through the window.

The families get in their cars and leave the parking lot as the bus disappeared in the distance. Cap stands in the middle of the aisle at the front of the bus to address the troops. Alright soldiers, listen up! We will be at the air strip in less than 5 minutes, when we get there make sure you use the latrine; we have a lot of shit to load on the C 1-30.

The plane has cargo net seats; so it's going to be a long uncomfortable ride troops. Supply Sgt! Yes Sir! I need your guys to get the manifest and meet me at the rear when we get there for an inventory check. Roger that sir! Motor Pool Sgt! Yes Sir! Stand by; I will get you guys loaded after inventory. Roger that Cap! Hey Doc! Yes Cap! Set up a tent by the hangar so we can give these soldiers their shots; don't need any troops getting sick. Gotcha Cap!

LT! Yeah Cap! Set up the class room in the hangar so we can give the troops a safety briefing after they've gotten all their shots. Got you covered Cap! Soldiers, we are going to Thailand on a Peace Treaty, we will not need to carry our weapons while we are there; so once we get to Camp Friendship we will be collecting weapons at first formation. Yall got that! Yes Sir! Well sound off then! Who Rah! All the troops shouted.

Good deal, let's have a fun and safe trip and make our country proud. Cap finished speaking then takes his seat as the bus enters the air strip.

The large Silver 200 passenger bus came to a stop in front of the hangar. LT stands up. Ok soldiers; unload and let's get information so we can take a head count. Yes Sir! The soldiers shouted and proceeded to unload the bus and form a formation in front of the hangar. LT called them to attention and started row call. Each soldier sounded off as he shouted their name. He looks over towards Cap. All accounted for sir! Thanks LT!

LT then faced the soldiers and shouted. Ok troops; time for shots and your safety briefing, unload your duffle bags and make it happen! Your briefing will be at 1800 hours. Yes Sir! The troops shouted. Lt;

standing at attention, faced the soldiers and shouted. Formation! Dismissed!

He and Cap made their way over to the Medic's tent to receive their shots, about ten minutes after; all the troops had assembled a line to receive theirs also.

The evening was warm and humid, an uncomfortable mix for the soldiers in full gear. The combination of wool socks, standard under garments, battle dressed uniforms and leather boots made the weather feel like the enemy. Several troops removed their BDU tops and wore only a brown military issued T-shirt to become more comfortable.

The hangar seemed to be out in the middle of nowhere, no cars, houses, people or other planes were in sight. Runway lights illuminated the strip as the sun went down and night fell.

At the rear of the huge oversized C-130 Aircraft, the supply Sgt. finished up his inventory and loaded the last pallet of goods. The motor pool Sgt. was assisting his troops with tying down the vehicles. Both Sergeants completed the task at hand, looked over everything twice to make sure it was up to standards then with their troops; joined the others in the hangar for the safety briefing.

Tim and Jeron stood at the front of the classroom in front of the projector screen. Specialist Cooper can you turn the lights off please? Cooper was standing against the dull grey wall at the back of the classroom. Yes sir! He turned off the lights. Several soldiers leaned over and placed their heads down on the desk in front of them.

Cooper! Cap yelled. Yes sir! Turn them back on! Yes sir! Ok soldiers, listen the fuck up! This is no time to be taking a nap, so pay attention. If I see anyone sleeping, you're bringing your happy ass up here and you're giving me 200 push-ups! You got that! Yes Sir! The troops shouted. Cooper, Lights! Yes sir! Corporal Brown, start the projector. Yes sir! Ok gentlemen; we are about to watch slides of some Std's that you can catch while over in Thailand, which is by the way, in the top five countries for Aids.

Trust me soldiers; you don't want any of this shit! If you catch anything we're leaving your monkey ass in Thailand. My advice to you; would be to keep your dick in your pants! The first slide came upon the screen. Damn! The soldiers shouted.

A disgusting picture of a penis with a swollen head in the shape of a cauliflower was on the screen. Gentlemen, this is what we call cauliflower dick; don't be a victim, keep your shit in your pants. Damn that's nasty! A soldier in the front row shouted.

Brown, next slide please! The next slide came up. Whoa! The room shouted. On the screen was a man's scrotum sack, the size of a basketball. Now I don't know what the fuck this is called but you get the message. Don't you gentlemen! Yes Sir! What's the message? Keep your dick in your pants! The room shouted. Good! Cooper, turn the lights back on please! Brown turn that shit off! Now, just in case some of you knuckle heads want to be hard headed, we have plenty of condoms on the med truck. Woo Ha! The troops shouted.

Ha-ha. Cap laughed at his troops. Excuse me sir! One of the soldiers in the back raised his hand. Yes soldier. How do the girls look over there? I heard they were beautiful. Yes they are some very pretty woman over there, just be sure you check for an Adam's apple. Excuse me sir! Let's just say, everybody that looks like a woman aint a woman solider! You understand! Oh, yes sir!

Sir! Sir! Another soldier shouted for his attention. Yes soldier! When are we going to be able to use the phone and how long is the flight? The flight is 18 hours, we have a fuel stop in Japan after 10 hours then we hit Karat, Thailand. The phone call, I'm not so sure. You might want to start writing a letter soldier. Ha-ha. The other soldiers laugh.

Alright troops, go take a latrine break and get geared up to board the C-130, dinner will be served on the flight. Woo Ha! What's for dinner Cap! MRE's soldier, what else! Awww Shit! The troops shouted. Ha-ha. Cap laughs as the troops head out to the strip to board the C-130.

8, Shacking up.

Simone and Tonya are having sushi in Manhattan. Patrons congest the sidewalk as they scatter about Times Square on their lunch break. The sister's occupy a few seats on the patio adjacent to the walkway. Cars and Taxi's alike lay on their horns as Bike-messenger's weave in and out of the congested traffic on the city streets.

Simone, I don't know why you like this swanky ass Sushi bar. Look at all these damn people and this loud ass traffic, girl; you need to find another sushi bar. Tonya, shut up and eat your California roll already. You so damn picky; with your high class ass!

Thump! What the hell! I know you didn't just throw that shrimp at me. Ha-ha. Tonya laughed at her sister's reaction. Yes I did and I'm not picky, so stop saying that. Yeah whatever! Bitch, your ass is high maintenance. Ha-ha. They both laugh then take a shot of sake. Tonya picked up her chop sticks to eat her roll. Ummmm. This is good sushi though sis. I know it is! Have you spoken with Lisa today? Yeah, I spoke with her right before I came here to meet you. How is she? She's doing ok, she just miss Scott's crazy ass.

I still can't believe that fool was drinking anyway. Me either sis! Simone said as she picked up her cucumber shrimp roll and dipped it in her soy sauce. Oh! Guess what sis! What is it Simone? Girl I got approved for the condo. Oh snap, when you moving in! Shit, at the end of the month. Well good for you baby; did you tell mom yet?

Nope! Why not! I want to wait until they get back home, if I tell her now she will try and make me stay at the house. Yeah, you're probably right. Ring-Ring. Tonya's mobile phone ringed. Hello! Hi baby! Heyyyy Tim! How are you doing sugar?

I'm good baby; it's hotter than a motherfucker over here in Thailand! Really! Hell yeah, it's like 120 degrees. Damn, that is hot! Yep; so what's going on in the Big Apple? Not much, just sitting here having lunch with my sister. Oh that's what's up, tell Simone I said hi.

She takes the phone from her mouth to deliver the message. Hey Sis, Tim says hello! Oh Hi Tim! She shouted! Where's my man at! Girl be quiet, I'm talking to my man now. Ha-ha. I heard her, tell her he's coming to the phone when I get off.

Nah, she can wait. So do you miss me? Hell yeah, I miss you girl, I think about you every day. I can't wait to get back. Aww, I miss you too baby. How is everything at the Agency?

It's going great; I renewed a few contracts and got some new ones too. Good for you baby! Tim, I need to ask you something. What is it baby? Well my divorce is final and you and I are starting to get really serious. Yeah, go ahead, spit it out. It's just that I'm tired of sleeping alone and I want you to move in.

I don't know Tonya; how do the kids feel about that? Boy, I'm the Momma, they will be alright. Ha; you crazy! I don't mind baby, in fact I would love too! But! But what! I rather we talk to the kids first and let them know what's about to happen. Ok baby; we can do that.

See that's why I love your ass man, you always know what to say. I love you too girl, I look forward to moving in with you. Hey LT, can I talk man, damn you and Tonya gone be on the phone forever! Alright; hold tight man! Hey baby, I'm about to let Jeron get the phone. I will talk to you later ok. Ok baby! He hands him the phone. Hello! Hi Jeron! Hey Tonya, how are you; can I speak to Simone please? I'm fine and here she is.

Hi Big Daddy! Hey baby! I miss you! I miss your pretty ass too girl. So how do you like Thailand? It's cool; just have to get use to this damn smell. What smell? It smells like shit over here! What do you mean? Baby as soon as we got off the plane and the doors opened the scent hit us. Wow, are you serious?

Yep, it smells like some old taco meat or something. Ha-ha-ha. Nigga you stupid! She laughed repeatedly. So what's new with you baby? Oh, I got approved for a Condo yesterday.

Now that's good news, when do you move in? At the end of the month; are you moving with me? Sure baby, I want to hit that ass every night, break that condo in girl. You silly! Well it's time for me to hang up Simone; I have to give these troops a briefing. Ok Big Daddy, I love you, talk to you later. Ok, good bye baby. Cap places the satellite phone on the desk inside his quarters.

On Camp Friendship, the living quarters were old and rundown; after all they were post-Vietnam barracks. In the center of base the locals had set up tent city, a local market for the visiting soldiers. The engineers were busy at work building a 12 stall latrine that was made of plywood and heavy duty trash bags.

Six wood steps led up to a long platform that had six man made toilets on each side. Every stall had a 4x4 square piece of wood with a hole cut in the center that held a long black trash bag which ran about 8 feet deep. A make shift door secured each stall, so that you could have some privacy, on the back of the door was a toilet paper holder.

The smell of human waste, seem to intensify with the 120 degree heat, and the annoying flies had made a home in what they would call a paradise. On the other side of the yard another crew of engineers built a shower room inside an old concrete bath-house. They installed several shower heads to stream water from an old well that sat in the center. The well although decades old, still managed to hold plenty of rain water that the soldiers used to filter through the shower heads.

Green algae and gnats had made a home in and around the well. The Camp sat in the center of the Thailand city called Karat. Although a third world country the city was home to McDonalds, KFC, Dunkin Doughnuts and several other chains that were in the USA.

Cap and LT sat at a table by themselves in tent city waiting for their lunch. A local by the name of Cat, a Thai woman in her mid-20's about 5' 4" with bronze skin and long black hair was cooking the meal.

Fresh red and green peppers, wild onions and mangos sat in the center of the cooks table. Cat sliced up raw pieces of chicken which was caught from the yard and placed it on the table beside the vegetables.

She lit a fire in her home made pit that was surrounded by brick and covered with a steel mesh grill. Cat placed a large wok on the grill and added a few dashes of fresh olive oil in to the searing pan.

She proceeded to add the chop vegetables and chicken in the wok. A strong aroma from the sizzling stir fry created a dangerous mixture of gas as she added in her spices. The soldiers sitting under the tent started coughing uncontrollably as they ran away from the tent area.

Yo man! Fuck that, I'm not eating that shit! Hell nah, me either Cap, let's go downtown and get something. Tim and Jeron walked away from tent city and headed towards the front gates.

Beep-Beep! The took-took; blew at the two soldiers as they crossed the street to exit the base. The small three wheel vehicle was like a tricycle with a carriage on the rear powered by a motor.

Immediately outside the gates of Camp Friendship was the busy little city of Karat. The streets were congested with took-tooks, Mercedes taxi's and buses. Amidst the hot and humid climate an awful stench filled the air. A combination of raw meat, rotten vegetables and old sewer water was constant in the busy city; it created a smell that was unforgettable.

Jeron and Tim made their way down the city side walk, pass the butchers, vendors and store fronts. Man I'm hungry as hell, let's check this joint out right here man. Cap, you sure about that! Yeah man! Alright let's do it! They came to a stop and entered the restaurant to place an order.

Patrons filled the tables in the lobby area as a line of people formed at the counter to place their orders. Jeron and Tim stepped to the back of the line. Hey cap! What is it LT? This place must be pretty good huh? Why you say that? Look at all these damn people, shit, the food must be good! Yeah man, we'll see in a minute, won't we? Yep, what are you getting Cap? Probably some chicken, don't want to order any of that dog meat. Ha-ha. Man, you really think they eat dog? Boy, you must have not seen that meat in the front window. What meat! Cap stops, turns around and points toward the entrance.

Man, stop bullshitting! Go over and take a look, if you don't believe me LT! Tim leaves Cap at the front counter then walks over to the front window.

Tim made his way through the patrons that sat at the few tables that were in front of the window of sun dried meat. He gets closer to the table that sat against the greasy pane. Rows and rows of meat lined the surface stacked atop of one another. What looked like snakes, duck, rat and a dog's head sat there for all to see.

LT came to a slow walk as he approached the meat on the table. Well, I'll be damned! He picked up the snake. Hey Cap! He yells across the restaurant. Yo! Look man! I told your ass LT! He puts the snake back on the table. What the fuck! Tim yells out as he leans over the meat and pulls up an object from a bucket in the corner.

He brings the object up to his face for a closer look. A long bamboo stick was shoved up the center of the object. Two legs hung low, two arms were along-side it's narrow torso. Ohhh hell no! This….. This….. A damn monkey!

A small black and crispy chimpanzee sat on the stick on sale, along-side the other meats that were usually pets in the U'S. Ha-Ha. Cap, laughs at LT as he throws the monkey on a stick on the table and makes his way back over to the counter. See, that's why I'm getting chicken. Hello Sir! May I help you today! The short Thai lady asked as the two soldiers came up to order.

Yeah, can we get some chicken? Chicken, how many chicken you want? We got chicken leg, that ok? Yes Ma'am; that will be four chicken legs. Ok, Ok, Four legs for you! She picks up two small brown paper bags and placed them on the counter in front of them. She reaches in the oven and pulls out four sun dried chicken legs with the feet still attached.

Hey! Hey Ma'am! What is this! Chicken leg sir! No, no, no! These are feet! Ha-ha. LT laughs at Cap as he argues with the cashier. Sir, you say four chicken leg! This four chicken leg! That will be 8 bot sir! 8 bot! Cap, come on man, forget that crap; let's go to KFC by the mall.

Jeron reaches in his pants pocket then pulls out two bills and left them on the counter. The soldiers exit the restaurant and find themselves amongst the busy city and traffic once again.

Beep-Beep! Horns blew at pedestrians running across the narrow streets as they crossed from one side to the other. Two slim Thai gentlemen stood along-side a small pick-up truck just outside the restaurant.

Look LT, those fools aint got on any shoes; out here in these nasty ass streets. Shit, forget about the shoes! Look at those two motherfuckers coming to the truck! Damn! Two small fellows were both carrying a half of a pig on their shoulders as they approached the pick-up.

Man this is crazy, how far to KFC. It's just a block or two up the way LT, right by the mall. Cap, I don't see how people live like this every day; these are some unsanitary conditions brother.

Remember this is a third world country man, so they don't have all the amenities like we do back home. Yeah, I guess you're right, God bless America! You can say that again brother! Bap! Cap punches LT on the shoulder.

After walking a block and a half they finally arrive at the mall. Adjacent to the left of the entrance sat a KFC and on the other side was a Dunken Doughnuts. Hmmmm. Some real fried chicken! Ha-ha! Jeron laughs at Tim as he stands at the entrance of KFC.

They make their way inside to find a packed lobby and see several fellow soldiers indulging in a familiar American treat among the locals. Yo Cap! LT! The soldiers yelled out from the corner booth. Hey Troops! Cap and LT went over to join them.

Damn, how much chicken you need soldier? Man, we got like three buckets Cap! We tried to eat at the local restaurants but they had some crazy shit. Ha-ha! Yeah, we did the same thing Specialist Taylor. So you understand then LT. Yes I do!

You guys can have some of ours; we have plenty to go around. Thanks Taylor! The officers joined the other soldiers at the table. Hey Cap, I'm going to order me a coke, you want something. Yeah man, get me one too. Sure! Thanks LT! No problem Cap.

One of the three buckets sat on the table empty as the soldiers feasted on the chicken. The red and white paper barrel began to fill with the naked bones as they ate their way through the colonel's recipe. Hey Cap! What's up Taylor? Did you see that monkey on a stick in the window at the restaurant down the block? Shit, we went in that place, LT picked it up! Ha!

That's when we said fuck that and came down here. Yo these people eat some weird stuff dude. Man, I aint eating nothing they cook, I don't trust any of it. I'm with you LT! Taylor and LT give each other a pound. Hey Taylor, pass me those biscuits. Sure, here you go Cap. LT and Specialist Taylor reached in the bucket to get a few more pieces.

The three gentlemen sat there quiet as they continued to eat. The other soldiers had just finished their food. Damn that was good, time to head back to base and take a dump! Spencer you are forever shitting dude! Hey Taylor, don't hate on me because I gotta take a shit! Bye man, see you later! Alright LT, Cap! See you guys at the base.

Alright soldiers, be safe out there, don't walk down any dark alleys. Later Cap! LT looks up from the table and noticed the patrons all looking over at them.

He puts down his chicken leg, picks up some napkins and cleans his greasy palms. Yo Cap, look around man. What am I looking at LT? Look at these people eating, what do you see different?

As the two soldiers gazed over the lobby area, Taylor noticed something weird as well. Man I don't believe this, we're over here eating with our hands and these folk got knives and forks. Cap; they're eating chicken like it's steak man. Yeah I see that LT.

They must think we're animals eating with our hands. Specialist Taylor slide me that bucket over here. Yes Sir! I don't care what they think! I'm eating my damn chicken like we do at home. You crazy Cap! LT and Taylor reached in and grabbed some more chicken and joined Cap as they finished up their meal.

Hey LT, I heard Tonya asked you to move in with her when we get back. Yeah she did! So are you going to do it? Hell yeah, why not? Man you know your Mom told you not to shack up. Cap looks at him and smirks. Simone wants you to move in to her new condo too, doesn't she? She mentioned it, I told her I would but I'm getting my own place too.

Your own place! Yep! How come? LT we only have 60 days before we are out of the Army. What does that has to do with it? I don't know about you but after we open up our restaurant, I'm gonna have at least three girls my man.

Cap, your ass is a hoe! Dude I aint married and until then I'm gone be a hoe! Ha-ha. Whatever Casanova! On the serious side though, we need to find a building when we get back. Where are we going to find one, in the city or what?

I don't know LT; the city is high as fuck! I think we should try Long Island or maybe Harlem. Harlem! Yeah Harlem! Dude, you crazy! I aint putting nothing in Harlem world; boy! Hey; it was just an idea. Don't worry about it now, we will figure it out when we get back. We still need to get the money off base too.

Cap, LT and Taylor finish up most of the chicken and box up the rest to take with them. The locals watch them with disgust as the soldiers make their way out of the restaurant into the busy third world city.

The sun had set and night fell over the city of Karat. Gorgeous Thai woman roamed the streets as they made their way to local bars and pubs. The soldiers resisting temptation had somehow made their way back on to Camp Friendship.

Beep-Beep-Beep. As they walked on to base a huge white 4 ton truck was backed up over by the latrine area. Hey Cap, what are they doing over there? Oh the Thai's are picking up the trash bags of waste from the latrine. Yuk! What are they going to do with it? You really don't want to know Taylor.

Cap nothing will surprise me now Sir! Ok in that case, they buy our shit and use it to fertilize the rice fields. What the fuck! Are you serious? Yes I am Specialist; you wanted to know, so I told you. Damn that is some nasty shit Sir! Hey just wash off your rice before you cook it soldier. Ha-ha. LT laughs at them. Damn! Taylor shakes his head and walks to his barracks. Later Cap! LT! Alright Taylor!

Jeron, I got some Thai liquor stashed bro. Tim you're an alcoholic, where the fuck did you find some Thai liquor bruh? Hey, that lady cat got it for me. Ha-ha. You slick motherfucker you! The soldiers enter the barracks to get a drink and put an end to an adventurous evening.

9,Progression.

The night is warm and patrons crowd the lines over at Club Platinum. Craig is standing outside the entrance greeting customers as they come in to enjoy old school Wednesday's. The S.O.S band's "No One's Gonna Love You" has the dance floor filled with people.

Sonya; dressed in a light blue Prada dress and matching heels, looks flawless as she mingles with the people.

She moves through the crowd shaking hands and giving hugs to the regulars and new patrons alike. Two young guys standing by the bar were bobbing their heads to the music as she approached their area. "No one's gonna love you, the way I do, Nobody" "No one's gonna love you, the way I do, Nobody."

Hello Gentlemen, are you guys enjoying yourself? Yes Ma'am; thanks for asking!

You're welcome! Damn, you're looking good in that dress. I can lick you from head to toe right now. What did you say? You heard me. Sonya looked at him and started to blush. He winked his eye at her, grabbed her by the hand and pulled her close.

Hey stop it; my boyfriend is going to fuck you up. Does it look like I care about your nigga! What! She looks at him and smirks. You should, he owns the place. He slowly turned her around then pulled her close. Sonya's back was up against his chest; he leaned down and whispered in her ear. I'm sorry Miss; I didn't mean to offend you.

His right hand slid down her side to the end of her dress. She took her left hand and softly pushed it away but he resisted. Uhhh. Sonya released a quiet sigh. The soft touch of his finger-tips had found its way to the top of her vagina. She leaned back closer to his body and tilted her head back on his shoulder. The music had seemed to get louder by the moment.

"No one's gonna love you the way I do" "Nobody (I can love you better)" Sonya pushed away. Bap! She slaps him. Stop, I can't! She yells then quickly walks away from the gentlemen. Ha-ha. He and his friend stood there laughing as she straighten her dress and walked off.

Sonya disappeared into the crowd making her way through the crowd on the dance floor. Blue and Yellow strobe lights bounce off the ceiling and walls, you could see her blue dress shimmer as she approached Craig at the front door.

Hey baby, it looks good in here tonight. Yeah, we already have about 800 people in. That's what I'm talking about Daddy! Muah! Sonya kisses Craig on the cheek. Did you get to greet everyone baby? Oh yeah, I'm on my job baby.

Ok, that's my girl. Craig grabs her hand and holds it tight. Come on; let's go out front, I need some fresh air. The couple walks out to the front of the club; he reaches in his shirt pocket and pulls out a cigar. Here let me get it daddy. Sonya takes the lighter from him and lights the stogie.

Thanks sugar! He takes a long pull then exhales the smoke into the warm Manhattan air. Bright neon lights and flashy cars created an intoxicating atmosphere as patrons pack the lines into the club.

Beep-Beep! Yo, What up Craig! Hey what up brother, yall good! He shouts back to the guys, rolling slowly by the club. Yeah bro, we coming in! Alright man; see you on the inside. Come on baby; let's go in before these fools want a free pass. He and Sonya turn around and walk back in the club as the lines begin to fill quickly, signs of another successful night at Platinum. Muah! He kisses her on the cheek as they enter. Go finish mingling with crowd and I will go check on the Dj. Cool daddy; see you around. He went left; her right and they disappeared into the crowd.

A few days later, Tonya and Simone, find themselves unpacking boxes in an empty Condo. Dressed in their Westbury High sweats, Nike sneakers and armed with a mop, broom, Windex and house cleaner.

The 5th floor condo had wood panel floors from wall to wall, stainless steel kitchen appliances, two large picture windows over-looking the park and egg shell white walls through-out the 3 bedroom condo. Tonya filled the bucket with warm water as Simone wiped off the appliances. Hey sis, this is really nice; have you spoken to Jeron yet? Yeah, he's coming over later when he's done out processing.

Damn, he's not done yet! Tim finished up 14 days after they got back from Thailand. No, he had to wait for the new Captain to in-process so he could brief him. Oh, ok, so is he moving in our what? Hell yeah girl, my man is moving in. How are things working out with Tim being there now? Shit, it is working! You hear me! I hear you sis!

Jeron told me that they were going to look for a building this weekend for the restaurant. Tim did mention something about that yesterday. Tonya; can I ask you a question? Sure sis! Can either one of them fools cook; I'm saying, I aint taste nothing from either one of them!

Damn, me either child! Ha-ha-ha! They fell over the counter laughing. Alright; let's finish cleaning this place up, the movers will be here shortly. Girl; we need to make sure they can cook before we let them spend some money on a restaurant.

I'm gone ask Jeron to make me some dinner this week to see what he's working with. That sounds like a plan, I will ask Tim also. Ok that's a plan, what are you going to do with these damn white walls? Simone was down on her knees wiping the fridge as she looked up at Tonya. Not a damn thing, leave them white! Tonya pushed the wet mop towards her sister. Stop girl!

Don't curse at me Simone, I just asked if you were painting the walls. Pop! Ouch! She slapped Tonya on the ass with a wet cloth. Knock-Knock! Damn, you have company already? It's probably the movers. Who is it! A-1 Movers Ma'am, we have your furniture. Ok hold on, I'm coming! I'll get it sis, finish wiping. Hey fellas! Hello Ma'am, are you guys ready for us to unload the furniture? Yes honey, you guys can start.

Ok, we will be back up in a minute. The fellow grabbed his radio from his side. Hey Paul! Yeah what's up Steve? Go ahead and start unloading, its unit 556. Roger that! Ok, fellas, let's get this stuff moved! He yelled to his co-workers leaning against the truck.

The moving crew unlocked the rear of the truck and started unloading. Steve made his way back down stairs to assist the guys. Paul! What's up Steve? Man there's two fine ass woman up there boy! Damn, I swear if I wasn't married. Ha-ha. But you are playboy, so be nice. He pats Steve on the back as they walk towards the rear of the truck. Watch out, coming through! Two of the movers made their way down the ramp then up to the condo to deliver Simone's couch.

Ring-Ring-Ring! Hello! Hey Lisa! Hi Scott, how are you baby? Tired of this nasty ass food and all these dumb inmates! Well; you only have a few weeks left. Yeah I know but it seems like forever. Well; I miss you and can't wait for you to get home.

I miss you too Lisa, I have been jacking off to your picture every night. Aww, you miss my loving baby! Hell yeah! Really! I'm sitting here on the bed naked, rubbing my hand across my fat cat. Yeah I like that, rub it soft baby. Hmmmm. Ok papa, my fingers are on my clit now. Stick them inside your pussy baby and imagine it's me. Hmmmm. That feels so good. Do it slow baby. Slow. Yes, slow.

Now take them out of your wet pussy and put them in your mouth. Ok! Now suck on them and let me know how your vagina taste! Lisa slid her fingers in her mouth and licked around the tips and in between them. Hmmmmm. Taste so good. Yeah, what does it taste like baby? Like… Like… Honey baby.

Damn Lisa, I am so hard and horny right now girl. I want you! Oh yeah, you want me baby! Hell yeah! Beep-Beep. A tone interrupted their conversation. This call will end in the next 10 seconds. Damn, I can't wait to get out of here! Be safe baby, I will come visit you….. Click! "This call has ended, please hang up". Damn that's fucked up; they just cut him off like that! Lisa slammed down the phone, turned off the lights and went to bed.

At the corner Pizza joint, the air is filled with the aroma of fresh dough, vegetables and pasta sauce. Jeron and Tim occupied a corner table in front of the window as they looked through the local classifieds for vacant buildings. This isn't working bruh! What's not working J? Staying with Simone! Why not?

I'm accustom to having my own shit, staying with this chick is not gone cut it. Man you tripping; that is your girl right? Yeah but I'm still fucking Erin too. Man you're gonna be a hoe forever! Tell me why you're still boning that girl after she gave you crabs?

It's just something about pussy that drives me crazy. I got to have it bruh! Even still, Erin though? I know; I got it bad huh? Yep, you damn right you do! Simone is what you need man, leave Erin's STD ass alone fool. I don't know Tim, maybe you're right! You think!

I'm gone think on it some more. Yeah do that; now let's find us a place for this restaurant. Look, here's a space in Manhattan, it says prior restaurant for sale or lease. How much is it? $12,000.00 a month or $189,000.00 for sale! Write down the number, we can put that one on the list to look at. Is there any more listed? Yeah hold on a minute, let me write this number down.

Just tell me the number Tim, I can write it. Oh ok, 212-277-8888. Cool, now what else is there? Hmmmm, here's another one for lease in Nassau. Where in Nassau? Freeport! Ok, what's the number? It's 513-208-2222! Cool, let's find one more and we can go check them out. Alright, let see. Here's a good one by Chelsea Pier. How much is that one?

Shit, this motherfucker says; for lease only$28,000.00 a month. Damn, that shit must have all the equipment in it already and food too! Ha-ha! They both fall out laughing. So; are we checking it out or what J? Yeah put it down; we can go there last. Cool, I'm going to wash my hands then pay this check then we can leave. I'll be at the truck bro! Alright Tim!

Jeron gets up from the table and takes his ticket to the counter to pay. Here you go man, everything was good as always. Thank you sir! You're welcome; have a good day. He makes his way to the restroom to wash his hands before going out to the car.

Tim is out front leaning against the pick-up waiting for Jeron while smoking on a cigarette. Ok brother you can drive, let's go. J comes out and throws him the keys. Here you go! The guys took the top off the jeep and sat it in the back.

Man I can't wait to open this joint up! Me either bro! Do you think they're going to miss the money on base? Hell nah fool; I didn't even log that shit in. Sweet! You the man boy! Yep; now let's go check these places out so we can start making some cash. Roger that my man; Roger that! Jeron and Tim speed down the neighborhood street in route to the first building.

Ahhh fuck! Turn the jeep around man; it's starting to rain! Man fuck that Tim; it's only drizzling, it want last long. Fuck it! Let's go then! The gentlemen kept driving to their destination.

10, Union.

Cloudy skies over shadow the Long Island neighborhood of Westbury, rain drops fall like bullets as they hit the hot concrete and city bus windows. The bus came to a complete stop at the corner and opened its doors. Out stepped a fragile black male, dressed in a baggy blue jumper and brown timbs.

As the rain fell, he walked down the sidewalk drenching wet. Three houses later, Scott opened the gate and walked up the steps to his home. He took a pause, reached in his pocket and grabbed some smokes, lit the cigarette and went inside.

He could hear the radio playing Klymaxx loud in the kitchen as he entered the living room. Lisa was singing along with the music, unaware that Scott was in the house. "Men all pause when I walked into the room, The men all pause."

Ummmm! Ummmm! Lisa tried to scream but couldn't. Scott had snook up behind her and put his hands over her mouth. Lisa dressed only in her robe and slippers, was in a panic. She had no idea who had her from behind. Shut up and don't say a word, nod if you understand. She shook her head to say yes.

Scott bent Lisa over the kitchen table then proceeded to lift up her robe. Yeah, I've been waiting a long time for this! Ummm! Ummm! Lisa moaned. He unzipped his pants, took both hands and placed one on each butt cheek. She jerked and wiggled, trying to get away from who she thought was a rapist.

After one last try, Lisa succumbed to his progressions then fell effortlessly on the table. Yeah, you're gonna like this baby! I've been waiting months for this pussy! Scott! She yelled. Smack! Then hit him on his side as she tried to swing while bent over the table.

He ignored her, pushed her hand away, parted those juicy butt cheeks and slid inside. Uhhh! Uhhh! Yes, fuck me daddy! Fuck me, fuck me hard! Ooowww! I missed you so much Scotty. Yeah, you like that baby? You like that! She backed up on his penis as he pulled out. He grabbed her by the hair and pushed forward as she continued to moan. Ummm! Ummm! Yes! Yes!

Boom! A loud thunder roared and the house lights went out. Damn! They both shouted. These fucking lights always going out baby! Scott and Lisa stood there in the dark. He backed away with a hard dick. Lisa it's been a long time baby, I need to cum woman! Shut up daddy, I got you.

Scott felt his way through the dark and made it to the kitchen counter. Hey, I'm over here baby, by the counter. Oh! Oh! Damn that feels good! Lisa had made her way over to him and was on her knees giving him head.

Oh! Damn, that's it! I'm about to cum baby! Come on daddy, come on! Oh! Oh! Oh! Shiiiittttt! Uhhhh! Scott came in his wife's mouth. Ughh! Ughh! Lisa coughed and stood up to spit it in the trash by the counter. Thank you baby! Damn, a nigga needed that! She wiped her mouth after spitting then kissed Scott on the lips. Muah! Welcome home baby!

Ring-Ring-Ring! Hello, thanks for calling WCI, how may I help you? Hi this is Keith, can I speak with Tonya please? Sure, hold on Keith. The secretary puts him on hold and page Tonya. Tonya, line one, Tonya line one! She's not responding. Ring-Ring! The other line rings. Hi WCI, how can I help you? Inga, this is Tonya, I'm in the restroom take a message. Ok, yes Ma'am! She switches over to Keith. Hi, can you call back in 30 minutes; she's busy at the moment. Sure!

Damn it! I don't believe this shit! Tonya's in the restroom mad, yelling and pacing back and forth. She placed the white stick on the restroom counter then reached in her purse to get another test stick.

Ok God! Please let this thing come up negative! Tonya walks over to the toilet, lifts hers dress and peas over the stick once more. Ok, Ok, come on God, I need a blessing. She shakes the pregnancy test a few times then places it on the counter by the other one.

Damn, I swear, I don't need any more kids right now. I need to talk to some-one, this is driving me crazy. She picks up her cell to call Simone. Ring-Ring! Hello! Hey Sis, what's up? Hey girl, what are you doing? Bitch I'm at the office in the bathroom waiting on this pregnancy test. What! Bitch you prego! Girl the first test was positive, I'm about to look at the second one now; hold on! Damn! Aint this, a bitch! Yes sis, I'm fucking pregnant!

I need a drink; I will call you later Simone! Ok girl, are you going to keep it? I don't know; I need to talk to Tim. Alright call me back! Yeah ok! Tonya leaves the bathroom and heads to her office. Inga, cancel all my appointments for this evening. Yes Ma'am!

She pulls a glass from her office cabinet and opens the Crown, pours a cup and takes a seat behind her desk. Tonya leans back, takes a sip from the glass and spins the chair around to face the large picture window. An unusual calm came over her face as she gazed out at the cars passing by below. Tonya rested her right hand that was holding the glass, on her thigh. She took a deep breath, exhaled, spun the chair back around to the desk then placed her office phone on speaker.

Ring-Ring-Ring! Yo this is Tim, what's up? Hey baby, how are you? I'm good gorgeous, how's work? Well it was ok! What do you mean by that Tonya? Are you sitting down? Yeah, what's up? I don't know any other way to say this but to just say it. Ok, say it then baby! Tim, I'm pregnant! What! Are you serious! Yes! That's good news baby, what's wrong? Dude, I have enough rug rats running around.

I understand that Tonya but I don't have any and you're my lady…. Sooo….. Man, you got to be kidding; you want me to keep it! Hell yeah girl! We need to talk about this some more Tim. What's there to talk about Tonya? We need to talk about us and our future if I'm going to keep this baby! Ok I understand, when did you want to talk? We can sit down after work tonight. Alright, Jeron and I are heading over to the building to get an inspection in an hour. Ok, tell J I said hi, see you later! Ok baby!

Hey J! What's up bro, why are you yelling? I just got some good news man. Oh yeah, what was it? Tonya's pregnant! No shit, you're gonna have a little Tim running around this joint. Yep, I think so! What you mean? She wants to talk about it first. Oh boy, that's not good. Why you say that?

One or two things bro! She wants to have an abortion or a wedding ring! One or the other my man, trust me on that. Dude, what the fuck ever! What's up with Simone though? We cool, I'm about to find me an apartment though. What for man, you already living with Simone! You're a good guy Tim, me on the other hand, I needs me some pussy on the side bro!

So you're getting a place so you can whore around and bring some STD home to Simone! Man, I aint gone give her no damn STD, stop saying that shit. Ring-Ring-Ring! Answer the phone man! Bro I aint answering Tonya's phone, fuck hat. Ha-ha-ha. You crazy bro! Jeron laughed at him as he leaned against the kitchen counter.

Tim walked over to the fridge and grabbed two cold beers and tossed one to J. Thanks bro! You still crazy though! Nah, your ass is crazy for going to get an apartment just to whore around. What time is it? Let's go get this inspection for the restaurant already. Don't be trying to change the subject J. Look Tim, give it a rest will you? Oh I'm cool but you should at least tell Simone.

I'm going to tell her when the time is right, I promise. Yeah I hear you playboy, I hear you! Grab the keys off the counter and let's go handle this business. Jeron picks up the keys and the guy's head outside to the jeep. Erin must have some of that come back pussy nigga, she got you fucked up! Dude who said anything about Erin! Man that's why you want another place, so you can fuck that young white bitch. I know you bruh, I know you!

Man, shut your ass up and start the damn jeep already. Don't get mad at me because you whipped by a bitch with crabs. Did you even tell her she gave you the crabs? Jeron sat there silent. See that's the BS I'm talking about, dude get it together before someone gets fucked up bro! I'm gone handle it Tim, shut the fuck up and drive man, damn!

Skrrrrrr! Skrrrrr! Tim pressed the gas and pulled off from the curb. Damn nigga! What man! You made me waste my damn beer fool! Skrrrr! Tim peeled off again down the neighborhood street and on to the nearby express way.

Downtown Manhattan, the sky is dark and gloomy, neon lights from the sky scrapers and billboards illuminate the foggy atmosphere. All the lights are on inside Club Platinum, on the outside Sonya pulls up in a yellow taxi just in front of the club. She steps out wearing her red pumps, Parasuco jeans and red jacket, holding an umbrella in her right hand. In the other hand she held a bag of clothes and shoes she just picked up from Macy's.

Sonya ran to the club entrance trying to get inside before the rain came down. Craig was already inside doing inventory before ordering the weekly stock list. She placed the umbrella against the outside wall and opened the heavy black steel door. Bright white lights blinded her as she opened it; soft jazz music was playing in the background. Craig was no-where in sight, she placed her bags and umbrella on the bar then started calling for him.

Craig! Craig baby! Where are you! Simone walked towards the dance floor, headed to the VIP area. Still, there was no answer or sign of him. Crunch! What the fuck is this! Sonya stepped on something then looked down to see what it was.

There on the floor surrounding her feet were bunches and bunches of dried red rose pedals. Crunch! Crunch! She continued to follow the roses up the steps, where the roses were now small red candles. Smells of apple cinnamon filled the air as the candles lit up the walk way to the last VIP booth.

Sonya made her way down the candle lit walkway and found her-self once again surrounded by roses. Shear white curtains draped from the walls and hung over a blue suede couch. 24 bouquets of roses surrounded the VIP section, a dozen on each side. There sitting in the center of the couch was Craig, dressed in black slacks, dress shoes and a silk cream shirt.

Baby what is this, it's so nice! Is all this for me! Yes baby girl, come over here and have a seat beside me. Sonya made her way through the roses and around the glass table that held one big red box, wrapped with a white satin bow.

Sonya took a seat on the couch beside him. You look nice baby; put your feet up here on my lap. Hmmm, are these new shoes? Yeah, you like! Yeah they look like you. So what's the occasion Mr.? Why the roses, candles and what's in this box?

Well I was thinking about us a lot lately and decided that it was time. Time for what! Craig reached over to the table and picked up the box. Here open it! Ok! Ok! Let me hold it! Sonya got excited as he placed the huge box in her lap. She pulled the white bow, ripped off the wrapping paper, opened the lid then looked inside to find a smaller box.

Oh my God! Baby! Baby! Is this…. Is this… A ring! Yes it is! Craig got up from the couch, got down on one knee. Sonya, would you like to be my wife? Yes! Yes! Yes! I would be honored! He stands up and she jumps in his arms.

The newlyweds hugged and kissed each other out of pure joy. Soft jazz music played in the background, the shear curtains swayed over the couch as the air from the ac blew. Candle flames flickered as the rose pedals danced across the floor. A strong cent of cinnamon apples filled the air to complete the perfect atmosphere to a perfect night.

11, Reality Bites.

All is quiet tonight in Simone's condo as she lays on her King size bed naked, looking up at the ceiling fan spin. Soft sounds of water running in the shower and the motor from the fan creates a relaxing environment.

Amber lights float across her window pane lighting up the night sky. Tap! Tap! Simone turn to look as the light bugs clashed against the window. The shower stopped and you could hear the stall door open.

Hey baby! Yes Jeron! I don't see any condoms in the drawer; did we use them all? Yeah, I told you it was the last one the other day, remember? Oh yeah, I forgot! Damn! What's the problem, you don't think I'm clean or something!

 Nah, it's not that, I just like to be safe. Yeah, implying that I'm not! Simone, don't start tripping! Hold on Mister! I'm not tripping; it seems to me you have an issue.

Girl, I don't have any issues with you. Ok, so why do you need a condom to fuck me then? Are you fucking someone else besides me?

See Simone! Now you bugging! Answer the question J! Jeron standing in the door way naked had just got done drying off. Whap! Stop that bullshit! Boy, don't be throwing your wet towel at me; answer the question.

Come on, I'm a big girl, I can take it! We aint married nigga! Oh yeah, you a big girl huh! Yep! She rolled over and sat up on the edge of the bed. Jeron walked over and sat down beside her. Well, spit it out sir! How many bitches are you sleeping with? He placed his elbows on his knees and hands to his face.

Simone, we only have been living together for a few weeks and you tripping already. She looked at him and raised her left eye brow, saying not a word.

Ok! Fuck it! There is this one girl I was messing around with before I met you. Are you still sleeping with her? I did a few weeks ago! Is it over with; are you still sleeping with her? I slept with her a few weeks ago and that was the last time. Damn J! Did you use a rubber with her?

He went silent. J! Well I was going to but she kind of jumped on me before I could get one. Oh hell nah! Simone became irate. I've been sucking on your nasty dick and you're out here sleeping around raw!

Calm down baby, calm down. No, you calm down! Did you go get checked for STD's, at least J? Jeron! Yeah, I did! Well, what were the results? It was nothing big. Nothing big! Simone stood up angry and shouting. What the fuck was it? She gave me crabs baby. Man you got to be fucking kidding me! How long ago was this?

About three weeks ago! Jeron, you are so damn sorry for that shit. Simone sat back on the bed and shook her head in disbelief.

I got it cured as soon as I found out baby. I stayed away from you until it was all cleared up. Yeah whatever, your ass aint getting none for a month! Take your sorry ass to the store and get some condoms! I'm sorry baby! I'm good J, as long as you didn't give me shit.

If you're going to be living with me, you have to cut all your hoes lose. It's gone be me and only me or you can get the fuck out! Yeah I here you Simone! You better do more than just hear me nigga! Ring-Ring! Damn who the hell is this! Hello! Hey Mone, this is Lisa. Hey girl what's up!

Jeron lay down on the bed as Simone took the cordless phone and headed up front. Girl, are you sitting down? No I'm in the kitchen. You need to sit down for this news baby. Ok, I'm sitting down, go ahead already! She took a seat at the kitchen table.

Well Scott came home a few hours ago and told me that your boy is back in town. What boy! Your ex, bitch; he's moving back and just got a job at the shop with Scott!

Get the hell out of here! I'm serious Simone! Hey what's wrong honey? Jeron walked in the kitchen and asked her. Nothing baby I'm alright. Where are you going? I'm going to the store to get those rubbers and a beer; did you want anything? Yeah, some Malibu! Ok, be back in a few.

Simone went back to her phone conversation. What else did he say Lisa? He asked Scott where you was, he wants you back! Shit, the devil is a lie! That fool still has three years left on his military contract, he aint moving nowhere. Baby, I'm just telling you what Scotty told me. Well, let me put on some clothes, I will call you back in a few. Ok Girl, later! What did she say baby, did you tell her?

Yeah Scott, I told her! She said he aint moving nowhere because he has three years left on his military contract. Shit, that fool already moved, we unloaded his furniture today! Oh well, I told her, it's on her now. Lisa walked over to the kitchen and grabbed the bottle of gin she kept on the counter.

Damn girl, you can't go a damn hour without drinking! Shut the hell up Scott! I can drink, you can't! Well, aint this a bitch, that's how you're gonna do me Lisa! Some kind of wife you are! Man I'm not trying to hear all of that, I can handle my liquor. You're the one that's in AA and trying to stay sober. Why should I suffer?

I'm not telling you to suffer, just have some respect and keep that stuff away from me. Yeah, ok! Lisa sat down at the kitchen table and poured herself a drink. Get you a glass Scott and have a seat! Ha-ha! That aint funny! Ok baby, damn, can I finish this one drink and I will put it up.

Scott walked over to his wife and kissed her on the cheek. Muah! Thanks baby, I'm going out back to change this oil. Ok honey, I'm going to pull out something for dinner. Smack! Scott popped her on the ass and headed outside. Hey bake some of those cookies too! Sure honey, peanut butter or chocolate chip? Peanut butter! Alright, I got you. Thanks baby!

As he headed out the door, she finished her glass of gin and poured another. Lisa quickly finished her second glass then poured a third. The bottle was close to empty as she turned up her third glass. Bam! She slammed the empty glass on the table, looked at the bottle, picked it up then put it up to her mouth to finish it off.

Ahhhhh! Damn that was good! Lisa shouted as she got up from the table and made her way to the stove. Two empty pots sat on the two back eyes; she turned them both on medium, took the silver can of grease from the counter and poured a half of a cup in each.

The pots heated at a slow pace as she walked to the freezer to pull out some chicken breast. Hey baby! Scott shouted from the backyard. Yeah hun! Bring me some water please! Ok baby, lemme put this meat in some water so it can thaw first. Ok! Lisa ran some water in the sink and sat the frozen chicken in it. Then pulled a bottle of water from the fridge and headed outside to Scott.

She walks on to the back porch and down the steps. Here you go honey! He leaves the car and walks over to Lisa. Thanks baby! Damn it's hot out here! Shit, you're sweating like crazy woman! Lisa took her left hand and wiped her forehead. The sky blue sun dress she wore was wet in front from perspiration.

Give me some of that water honey; you need to hurry and finish with this car. It's too hot out! Girl it aint that damn hot, its night time; it's that damn alcohol you just drunk up! What did you mean by that Scott! Did you drink just one glass or the whole bottle? Ha-ha! She laughed as she put her hands on her hips. Well answer the question? What do you think? I think you finished the bottle; in fact, I bet my life on it!

What the hell ever Scott! I'm just saying baby, I know you! Beep-Beep-Beep! What's that noise Lisa? Beep-Beep-Beep! There it is again! Beep-Beep-Beep! Both of them stood at the bottom of the steps trying to place the noise.

Beep-Beep-Beep! It's coming from the kitchen baby! Scott ran up the steps and went inside as Lisa stood there confused. What the fuck! Girl you done set the stove on fire! He rushed inside to get the fire extinguisher from the cabinet under the sink. The flames from the two pots had reached the hood over the stove as smoke filled the kitchen.

Scott unpinned the extinguisher and sprayed the blazing fire. Lisa walked in the house, her face hung in shame. I'm sorry honey; I must have turned the stove on by mistake. No, your ass is drunk, that's why! You almost burned our damn house down, I'm glad I changed the batteries in the smoke detectors last week.

Come on let's get this smoke out of here. The couple opened every window and door in the house to let the smoke escape. You're so damn drunk; you tried to fry the chicken with nothing in the damn pot. Hell the fucking chicken is in the sink thawing. You need to go to one of my meetings; this is crazy.

Lisa walked over beside him, looked in his eyes, kissed him on the lips then said. Fuck you and that damn class; you're the alcoholic not me! Yeah, at least I never tried to burn our house down. Whatever Scott; take your ass back outside! Fuck you Lisa! She walked out the front door as he stood in the kitchen. Yeah stay your ass out there and cool off; you damn drunk! She opens the door and sticks her head in. Fuck you Scotty! Recovering Alcoholic; go to a damn meeting already! Slam! She slams the door.

Scotty just looks at her and shakes his head then thought to himself. Damn; that used to be me! He reached in the fridge;

grabbed a beer and headed back out to the back yard.

The next day; Tim and Tonya are sitting by the park fountains just off Prospect Avenue. Young boys and girls alike run back and forth under the park sprinklers to relieve themselves from the summer heat. The couple; watch the kids play as they discuss their near future.

Tim I sure hope you're going to be committed because if you're not and you leave me stuck with another rug rat! Boy! Tonya looks at him and shakes her head. Why you looking at me like that woman? Why do you think? Look baby, I love you and I aint going no damn where. Get that through your head will yah? I hear you man! I hear yah!

All I'm saying is, if you start tripping; I got a 357 for your ass and let me assure you, that my daddy, taught me how to shoot, real good! Ha-ha! Girl you crazy! Yep, you damn right and don't forget it! Got me sitting here with my stomach popped out, because you want a baby!

Come here gorgeous! Tim pulled her closer and gave her a kiss. Muah! You know I love you right? Yeah, you better and by the way. How is the restaurant coming along? Oh it's getting there; we passed the inspection, now we have to get all of our licensing from Nassau County.

Nassau! Yes! Oh so you guys decided to go with the building in Freeport? Yeah it made the most since, we kind of wanted a neighborhood establishment. Oh that's great baby but I have one question. What's that baby? Can you or Jeron even cook? I'm just saying me nor my sister haven't taste as much as a sandwich from either of you. Ha-ha! Go to hell Tonya! Ha-ha! Baby I'm serious; people want good food don't they? Yes they do!

That's all I'm saying! Can your ass cook? Yeah girl, a little! A little, see that's that bullshit! Boy, how are you fools going to open a restaurant and you can't cook. We already took care of that problem baby. Oh yeah, how so? Jeron's Dad is a Master Chef and he's moving down from Carolina next week to run the kitchen.

Oh really! Yep! See, we got this! Ok, ok, maybe you do. I want some ice cream honey, how about you. You want some? Sure I could go for a banana split right now. Cool, let me get these rug rats. Tonya stood up and called for the little ones. D! Come on get your brother and your sisters and let's go. No mommy! Boy; come on here! We're going to get ice cream. Yay! Ok! D ran back to the sprinklers to get his sisters and twin brother.

Tim leaned down to pick up the towels off the edge of the fountain. The kids came running over full of energy and laughter. Yay, can I have a cone mommy? Yes baby girl, come dry off so we can get in the car. Tonya took a towel from Tim and proceeded to dry off her daughters. The twins took their towels from him and dried themselves.

The ready-made family, grouped up and headed away from the park and over to the car that was parked by the curb. They approached the car; Tim unlocked the doors and went to place the wet towels in the trunk. The twins and Karen jumped in the back seat first then Tonya buckled baby girl in her car seat. After she got the kids in safely she sat down in the passenger's seat as Tim started the car.

The family of six plus one on the way, pulled away from the curb and headed up Prospect Avenue toward the ice cream parlor.

Ring-Ring-Ring. Baby is that your phone? Nah my battery is dead. Ring-Ring! Damn, must be mine's then. She picked her purse up off the floor to get the cell. Hello! Hey Tonya, it's Craig! Yeah what is it? The detective called and said that they found your gun; he's bringing it by my place tomorrow.

Ok that's cool, just drop it off at the office, I will be there late tomorrow evening. Ok will do! Thanks, bye! Hey baby! Yeah, what's up Sonya? I just got done counting the receipts from this weekend. Alright, give me ten minutes to finish counting this door money and I'll be around there. Ok honey, you want a drink? Sure, let me get a Crown and coke. Ok!

Sonya got up from the kitchen bar and headed over to the liquor cabinet. The 6 foot tall, cherry oak wood cabinet, consisted of six shelves and two glass doors. The first shelf held the Crown, Makers, Hennessy, Jack Daniels and Paul. On the second sat Absolute, Kettle One, Goose, Smirnoff and Belvedere. The third shelf held a few shot glasses, Champagne flutes, Beer mugs and Rocks glasses.

Sonya opened the doors and reached for the Crown off the top shelf. She; then pulled a bottle of Jose' from the fourth shelf; which also held the Seagram's and Tanqueray Gin. Baby! Yeah honey! Come here! Hold on; let me finish the drinks!

Fuck them drinks; get in here! Alright, alright I'm coming! She put the bottles down and ran to the bedroom. Holy shit! What the hell is all this! Wooh! Hoo! Sonya screamed as she stood there and watched Craig throw tons and tons of money in the air.

The bedroom floor as well as the king size bed was covered with money. Craig kept digging in a blue duffle bag that sat at the edge of the bed and throwing up more and more money. Baby is all this from the club! Yes! We made 47 gees at the door last night! Wow! Are you kidding! Does it look like I'm kidding! Ha-ha! He laughed as he stopped throwing the money then fell on to the bed.

Oh my God baby; this means we made $70, 000.00 last night! What girl, I said

$47,000.00 where did you get 70 gees? After I deducted stock cost from the receipts we had $27,000.00 left in profits. So that means we made $70,000.00 in profits. Yes! Yes! Yes! Craig shouted as he rolled in the bed of money.

Oh my God; I am so horny right now baby! All this fucking money; we made in one night! I want to have sex in it daddy! Come here then girl and let me tap that wet pussy! Ummmm! I'm coming! Sonya took off her T-shirt and shorts then jumped in bed with Craig and his money.

As she fell back on the bed, her caramel tone legs bounced up in the air as she slid closer to him. Craig reached down with his left hand and slowly but gently rubbed her soft, wet vagina. A sensual peace came over Sonya as she lay there submitting to his every stroke. Her back arched off the bed, hands gripped a fist full of money and she spread her legs wider apart. Craig slid down to the edge of his bed to her feet.

Put one hand on each ankle then pulled her pelvis up to his mouth as he kneeled at the foot of the bed. The heel of Sonya's feet barely grasped the edge of the bed as he moved in to kiss her juicy vagina lips. Ummmm-Ummmm. That feels so damn good honey. You like that baby, you like that? Yes, eat that pussy daddy, eat it. Slurp---Slurp---Slurp. He licked the inside of her creamy walls then sucked on the clit.

In a circular motion he went, counter clockwise then back to the right, inside then outside then in again with a strong stroke of the tongue. Uhhhhhh! Uhhhhhh! Damn baby, you're eating the fuck out of my pussy! Oh! Oh! Oh! Oh! The sheets began to slip off the edges as she clinched hands full of money and comforter simultaneously.

Slurp---Slurp---Slurp. Oh my God! This feels so good! Oh! Oh! Don't stop, please don't! Ohhh yeah, right there, that's the spot daddy! Craig took his erect tongue and went from the bottom inside of her fat cat to the top, right under the G-spot.

Oh! Oh! Oh! Motherfucker I'm Cumming! Oh! Oh! He kept stroking her G-spot strongly with his tongue until her body collapsed and juices flowed down her throbbing vagina on to the dirty, stinky pile of money.

12, I Love you.

Jeron and Simone are sitting home alone watching TV when the phone rings. Ring-Ring-Ring. Hello! Can I speak to Jeron? Yes this is Jeron! Hey baby! Excuse me, who is this? This is Erin man, stop playing. Who? Oh; you're an owl now huh? Erin! J jumped up from the couch and walked in to the kitchen.

Simone looks at him confused. Where are you going? I'm getting something from the kitchen! Ummm Hmmm; don't get fucked up in here J! He ignores her and keeps walking while talking in a soft whisper. Erin; why in the hell did you call here! I told you to only call during the week between noon and 5! I know but I miss you and you were not answering your cell. Girl you are losing your fucking mind right now.

I'm hanging up this phone; I will talk to you tomorrow. No don't! Erin, stop bugging! No I want to see you tonight; come over, please! Ok I will, I have to go! Simone is in the other room, bye! J, don't hang up! Click! He walks back up front to watch TV. Who was that baby? Ahh nobody; just had the wrong number. Yeah right, stop lying!

I'm serious baby! So what did you get out of the kitchen? Uhh-Uhh-Uhh! Oh I forgot it! Ring-Ring-Ring! He reaches for the phone he placed on the arm of the couch. Bap! Ouch! She slapped his hand and picked up the phone. Ring-Ring! Hello! No one answered. Hello! Still no answer!

Click! Who was that! Nobody, some fool playing on the phone. They never said anything. Oh! I'm going to get that beer I left on the counter, did you want anything? Yeah, fix me a ham and cheese! Ok, be right back baby! Ummm Hmmm. Jeron left the room to fix her sandwich and get his beer. Simone still didn't feel right about the last ten minutes of events. She sat there puzzled, tapping her feet and rolling her hair around her right pointer finger. Fuck it! She shouted then picked up the phone.

She looked at the receiver then pressed star then 6-9. Ring-Ring-Ring! No answer but she didn't hang up. Ring-Ring-Ring! "Hi you have reached Erin, sorry I can't take your call right now but leave a name and number and I will hit you back." Click! She hung up the phone and her face now had a serious snarl. Jeron made his way back with the beer and sandwich. Here you go babe! She snatched the ham and cheese from him. Damn, what's wrong with you?

What! I said, what's wrong with you? He repeated himself then took a sip from his beer can while looking at her. Who the fuck is Erin? Who is she J? Ugh- Ugh! He almost choked on his beer when she asked. Girl, what are you talking about? The bitch that called here earlier and you said they had the wrong number! Man you tripping; don't start this crazy shit today, damn Simone! She looked at him and raised her left eye brow with a serious stare.

Don't get fucked up in here Jeron! I will put a bullet in your ass, I aint the one. Girl, eat your sandwich and stop that nonsense. Well I think you're lying, I can see it in your face; you almost choked when I said the bitch name! Look Simone; are you gone let that nonsense go or what? Or what!

Ha-ha! You got jokes huh! See; that's why I'm getting my own shit, you crazy! You damn right and don't you forget it! J jumps up from the couch, takes his beer and headed for the door. Where you going Jeron? To the damn store, away from your crazy ass! Bam! He slams the door behind him. Fuck you then! She yelled.

Ring-Ring-Ring! Hello! Hey sis! Hey Tonya, what's up? Working late; what you doing? Mad, watching TV! Mad for what? It's nothing me and J just had an argument. Oh, I know how that is. Yeah, anyway why you working so late? Girl, my assistant is on vacation and I have to pick up the slack by myself. Damn, why you aint call me to help. I forgot all about it; it's no big deal though. Oh, ok.

Anyways can you do me a favor and take the kids something to eat. I want be home for another two hours. Sure sis, I got you. Ok babe, thanks, chat with you later. Bye girl. Inga! Inga! Yes Ma'am! Can you bring me a cup of coffee and that blue folder off the table in the conference room? Yes Ma'am! Thank you sugar!

Tons and tons of 8 x 10 glossy photos of male and female models covered the floor. She sat there in the middle of the chaos, searching for new talent to bring to her company. Here's the folder and your coffee Ma'am. Thanks Inga, sit the coffee on the desk and hand me the folder.

Ok Ma'am! Tonya opened the folder to review the resume's that assisted the pictures. Ok Inga, I think I found a few candidates; here, take these eight pictures and read the names out. Ok!

Maurice McCoy, Diana Brown, Kevin O'Hara, Chrissie Lions, Rachel Keith, Melanie Scott, Brian Gray and Timothy

Green! Alright, here are the resume's to match the names, paper clip them together and put them on the conference room table. You can go home after that's done; we have a long day tomorrow.

Ok Ms. Tonya! Inga left the office and headed to the conference room as Tonya started to collect the pictures off the floor. Ring-Ring-Ring! Damn it, whose calling at this hour? She reached up to get the phone off her desk. Hello, WCI! Hey gorgeous! Hey Tim; what you doing baby?

I'm in the limo headed your way! Limo! Yes! For what! It's a surprise; just be ready; I'm 15 minutes out! Ok sugar; you're so crazy! A big smile came over her face as she hung up the phone. Inga! Yes Ma'am! Are you done? Inga walked over to Tonya's office door with purse in hand.

Yeah, I was just about to leave. Ok, have a good night lady; see you in the morning. Alright, good night Ma'am! She headed for the exit as Tonya followed behind to lock up. The office was quiet and empty, she walked the entire floor to make sure all the windows were locked and lights were off.

 Ring-Ring-Ring! Hello, WCl! Come on baby, I'm down stairs. Be there in a minute baby, locking up! Tonya walked to the front door and keyed in the security code to set the alarm. Beep! The alarm sounded and she exited her Manhattan office. Just outside her door and waiting by the curb sat a shiny onyx limo with dark tinted windows.

The back door came open and Tim stepped out. Come on Gorgeous, get in! Tonya dressed in blue pin striped slacks and satin white blouse, stood there, hair pinned up and both hands in her pants pockets. What are you up to Mister? It's a surprise woman; come on, let's go. She looked at him and smiled, full of excitement.

After you my dear lady! He stepped aside and showed her in. Tonya got in and took a seat in the rear of the limo. Tim closed the door and joined her; he then reached for a bottle of champagne from the limo's bar. What kind of Champagne is that baby? I don't drink anything you know! Girl I got this; just set back and relax.

Well, excuse me Casanova! Ha-ha! Yep, that's right Casanova. Ha-ha! Whatever Tim; where are the glasses? Right there beside you in that cabinet. Right here! She turned and pointed at the cabinet. Yes baby; get two glasses please. Ok honey; you still didn't tell me what kind of bubbly that is? It's Dom baby! Oh cool; my favorite! Here you go; pour up!

The Limo slowly pulled away from the curb and traveled through the busy, neon lit streets of the big apple. Tim filled both the glasses and they sat back to sip there drinks. The limo pulled off the street and entered the parking garage of a downtown building. Baby where are we going?

Drink your champagne baby; you will see shortly. Ughhhhh! I hate surprises! The limo slowed down and came to a stop at the top of the building. There was a loud humming sound and what felt like wind shook the limo. Baby! Baby! Why is the damn car shaking? Ha-ha. Calm down woman; it's cool.

Tim opened the door then reached for her hand. Come on; let's go gorgeous. She took his hand and exited the vehicle. Oh My Freaking God! You didn't! Why is that helicopter here? We're going for a ride my love! Hold your head down and stay close to me. The two held their heads down and ran to the chopper. Oh baby; I am so nervous! Why baby? Because! Because what? This is my first time on one of these! Oh it's not bad; come on.

They take a seat in the chopper and buckled their seat belts. The night was clear as the chopper lifted up towards the clear New York City sky. Have you ever taken a tour of the City this way; amongst the clear night sky? No, first time; it looks so pretty up here. The Big Apple skyline captured the night air like a portrait that sat calmly amidst the still black water.

Off in the distance you could see the beautiful Statue of Liberty and all her glory. Look Baby; that is so gorgeous! Yes it is; did you want to go closer? Yeah; let's do it! Excuse me sir! Yes sir! The Pilot answered. Can we get a closer look at the Statue of Liberty? Sure; no problem man. Great; thanks brother!

Tonya was busy looking at the city from the side window as they approached the Lady Liberty. Tim reached in his pocket with his right hand and unbuckled his seat belt with the other. A bright light shined through the chopper windows as they came upon this awesome beauty. Look Tonya; we're here! She was still looking out of the side window when they approached the statue.

Oh My God! Tim! Tim! Tim! Her eyes began to tear up as she watched this thing of beauty. Oh My God! She couldn't believe her eyes; there flapping in the wind and hanging down from Lady Liberty's torch was a white banner; that read in red letters. "Tonya; will You Marry Me?" Yes! Yes! Yes!

She turned to him with tears running down her face. Yes baby; Yes! Tim was now on one knee and took his hand from his pocket which held a ring. Tonya; will you be my Bride? Yes! Yes! She grabbed him by the cheeks and kissed him all over his face.

I love you so much Tim; you crazy fool! Ha-ha. I love you too gorgeous and I want to Love you forever. A strong gust of wind blew over the Atlantic; flapping the banner as it hung in the crisp night sky. The pilot rolled the chopper up and away from the Statue of Liberty and flew back towards the neon skyline as the couple caressed one another with joy. The red light on the tail of the chopper got dimmer and dimmer as it faded in the distance.

Beep-Beep-Beep! It's 2pm in the city the next day; the streets of Manhattan are busy and congested as usual. Cars, trucks and buses lay on their horns trying to cut their way through the chaos. Taxi! Taxi! Sonya and Craig yelled from the curb.

Daddy we're not getting a cab, it's too busy out here, aint shit moving. Ring-Ring! Sonya is that your phone? Ring-Ring! Yeah! Hello, this is Sonya. Hi Sonya; where the hell are you? What; who is this? This is David! Sorry you have the wrong number! Click! Who was that baby? Some crazy dude; thought I was someone else. Oh! We're not getting a cab man! This is crazy!

Fuck it; let's go somewhere and waste some time. Really, I have a place we can go daddy! Oh yeah, where might that be? Ahh, just up the block on 5th avenue! I should of known; with your shopping ass! Ha-ha!

Why are you laughing; come on let's go; please! Sonya pulled him by the arm away from the curb. Ok, ok; you're lucky I love you; let's go spend some money! Yes! Muah! She gave him a big kiss on the lips.

We only have an hour before we have to be at the club; so just one store; ok! Alright; that's cool; we'll just go to the Gucci store; it has everything we need! We, huh? Yeah daddy; they have shoes, ties, wallets, belts, clothes, all kinds of men's stuff! You're too funny!

The couple walk away from the curb and headed up the sidewalk towards 5th Avenue. In close proximity, you could see the bright gold trimmed building boasting its display windows that sat at the corner of 5th. Huge Gold letters stood out over the entrance and the display window that read GUCCI.

You could see rows and rows of ladies shoes inside from the side window. In the large display window; mannequins were dressed in men's suits and ladies evening wear. The couple approached the entrance. Ooohh look baby, I love that blue dress!

They entered the brightly lit store. Hello Folks, welcome to Gucci; is there anything special I can help you with? Yes; I want that dress! Sonya turned around and pointed at the mannequin in the display window. Sure; I can get that for you; come over here and let me see what size you need.

Sonya walked over to the sales person. What about you sir? Is there anything I can get you? Yeah but go ahead and help my fiancé; I can wait! Sure, as you wish; Ma'am, this way please. That one you're wearing is nice too! Thank you Ma'am; it's one of my favorites.

The ladies went to the dressing room as Craig continued to browse the show room floor. Another sales person seen him browsing and went over to assist; just as he started to look at the shoes. He picked up a pair of black leather ones with the signature buckle. Did you want to try those on sir? Craig looked back at the salesman. Yeah, sure why not!

Great; what size did you need? Oh, let me get it in a 10 ½. Sure, I will be right back.

Cool, take your time man. Hey baby! Sonya called out to him while standing outside of the dressing room. He turns around to see her. Damn! You look good baby! I like that one! See; I told you!

All you need now is some shoes to go with it! Ahhh; really baby! Yeah girl; might as well go all the way! Ma'am; can you find her some shoes to match the dress and some accessories as well. No problem sir; I will get right on it. Craig walked over to the counter to look at the display case of shades.

Ok sir; try these on and let's see how they fit. Cool! He sat down on the stool beside the display case and removed his shoes. The salesman slipped the leather ones on his feet. There you go sir; you can check them out in that mirror just over by the window.

Craig walked over to the mirror. They feel comfortable already! He looks at himself. Yeah; I like these; now I need something to wear with them; something new. A black suit would look great with them sir! You think so man! Yes I do! I tell you what brother; let me see what you got and while you're at it! Let me get those black shades and the silver ones for my lady.

No problem sir; I will get those for you right now. Thanks my man! It's no problem; can you wait for me by the dressing room; I will meet you over there with the suit. Cool! Craig walked over to the dressing room and took a seat on the bench just outside of the stalls.

Sonya and the sales lady walked out in front of him. Now; what do think baby? You look amazing honey; those shoes set it off! I'm about to try on a suit and I got us both some shades too. Awww; my baby getting a new suit! Yep! Here you are Sir! Oh; I have to go try this suit on; be right back! Go pick yourself out a necklace and get me a watch while I try this on. Ok daddy!

Sonya smiled at him as he walked away. Her face glowed with happiness and she had a bounce in her step as she walked to the display case. Ma'am; give me the most expensive watch for my fiancé and I will take the best-selling necklace you've got!

Yes Ma'am! I have just the watch; he will love it! Great; you get all that together; I'm going to take off this dress and shoes. Sonya went back to the dressing room to take off the dress as Craig was walking out. Oh shit! Look at you Mister! So how do I look baby? Just Like a damn model; you should wear suits more often!

That's what I like to hear! Alright my man; I'll take it! Great; I'm glad you like it sir! The salesman walked up behind him and removed his jacket. Both Sonya and Craig then walked to the dressing rooms to take off their new threads. The salesman waited for them outside the stalls so he could take the items up front.

The sales lady; rung up the shades, watch and necklace. Hey I already rung up these items; you just have to add in the suit, dress and shoes. Ok thanks! The salesman had just approached the counter. He totaled up the items and slid the dress and suit in separate bags.

The couple came up front to pay their bill. Alright my man; what's the damage? Ok Sir; let's see, the watch is $18,000.00, necklace $16,000.00; Men's shoes $7,000.00, ladies heels $9,000.00, dress $23,000.00, Tie and shirt $1,200.00 and suit $32,000.00. Your grand total is $106,200.00 sir! Oh no, that's wrong; I'm sorry; I forgot the shades! Let's see; the two pair of shades is $400 each; so your new total is $107,000.00! Will that be Visa, Master card or American Express Sir? Damn! Craig shook his head and reached in his back pocket for his wallet.

Here go my man; put it on the Visa and add $300 for your-self! Thank you sir! Yeah, you did a good job; you earned it! Baby! Baby! What honey? What about her; she helped us too! Oh, my bad baby! Add another $300 for her my man! Yes sir; your new total is $107,600.00! Ok, go ahead and swipe the card already before I change my mind! The salesman held his head down, picked up the card and swiped it. Here you are sir; sign here please!

Craig signs the receipts as the sales lady hand Sonya the bag with the watch, shades, necklace and shoes. Here you go man and thanks for everything! No thank you sir and here is the rest of your items. He handed Craig the Suit and Dress.

The sales lady walked the couple to the door and held it open for them. Thank you for shopping with us guys; have a great evening! The couple looked at the lady and smiled as they exited out the building. Thousands of people, cars, cabs and buses jammed the Manhattan streets. Craig and Sonya held hands as they walked down the busy side walk and disappeared among the crowd of New Yorkers.

Over on Long Island; Lisa and Scott are just sitting down in the kitchen to enjoy some fresh steamed shrimp. Two bottles of

Chardonnay sit on the table, one half empty, the other full. Damn sugar; I forgot the cocktail sauce! Can you get it please? Sure baby!

Scott got up from the table and made his way back over to the fridge. Did you need anything else baby? Nah, that's it; you better fix you some pop or some water or something. All I have over here is this wine. Oh yeah; let me take care of that. He reached back in the fridge and grabbed a can of cold coco cola.

Alright; now let's dig in to these shrimp! In the center of the table sat a large silver platter piled with shrimp and a glass bowl of cocktail sauce sat on the side. Lisa poured herself another glass of wine. Umm, these are seasoned good baby!

Thank you honey, I used my special recipe! Whatever girl; this is some damn Old Bay! Yep and some extra ingredients too! Ok, if you say so! Shut up and drink your coke! Ha-ha! You got jokes now I see! No baby; I was just saying have a drink because the shrimp are kind of spicy!

Lisa, if you're not going to respect my sobriety we're going to have problems. Scotty; look at me over here! Do I look scared or even worried about you giving me problems! She leaned back in the chair and turned up her glass of wine. You heard what the fuck I said woman!

Slam! Lisa slammed her glass down on the table as she brought her chair back to its up- right position. Scott, I'm not going to let you worry me today. Here! She slid the fresh bottle of Chardonnay over towards him. Open this and stop crying like a baby!

Nobody's crying; you just need to slow down on this damn drinking. Man, shut your face and open that wine already! Pop! Scott uncorked the bottle and pushed it back over to her. Thank you; did you want some?

Ha-Ha-Ha. Kiss my ass Lisa! He got up from the table and walked over to the fridge.

What are you getting from the fridge baby? A slice of cheese cake; did you want some? Sure; bring the dish over here. Scott grabbed the cheese cake then pulled a knife from the drawer and two plates from the cabinet.

Slam! Damn baby; slow your ass down. Lisa had finished another glass and slammed it on the table then poured another. I got this Husband; just cut me a piece of cheesecake! Ugh! Scotty sighed under his breath then slid Lisa a slice of cake.

She took a few sips of wine then proceeded to eat her cheesecake. Ummm; this is good! Scotty now upset at his wife for drinking so much, watched her eat the cake as he continued to eat some more shrimp. She took a sip of wine then a bite of cake.

Baby; why aren't you eating your cheese cake; it's good! I will eat it in a minute; I want to finish these shrimp first. Excuse me; suit yourself! She took another sip of wine.

Lisa; you really need to put that bottle away; you've had enough!

Man; I aint putting nothing away; I can drink all I want! Lisa turned up her glass and drink until it was empty. Slam! How you like that sir! This is my last time telling you; you've had enough! Fuck you Scotty! Ok that's it! He jumps up from the table, snatches the bottle and throws it in the garbage.

Stop; give me my wine! No; sit your ass down girl! He pushed her back down in the chair. Slap! Ouch! She smacked him in the back then reached for the trash can. What the hell are you doing woman! Get away from the damn garbage; you got a serious problem!

Move Scott; give me my wine! No; sit your ass down! He sits her back in the chair. You Motherfucker! Bing! What the fuck you do that for! Lisa threw her glass at him and it broke against the wall. You aint my daddy;

give me my damn wine nigga! Look; you need to calm your ass down!

Swoop! Ouch! Shit Bitch; is you fucking crazy! You're throwing knives and shit! Oh my God; baby; come here; you're bleeding. What? Where! Oh my God! Oh my God! Girl you're scaring me; what! Lisa ran to the counter and picked the dish cloth. What the hell are you doing with that? Baby you're bleeding!

Scott ran up front to look in the living room mirror. Oh shit! You crazy bitch; you cut my fucking ear off! Blood was dripping at an alarming rate from the left side of his face; where his ear used to be. God dammit! Call the ambulance! Oh my God; I'm sorry Scotty! Call them! Now! Ok! Ok!

Fuck! I'm gone die because of your drunk ass! Here baby; hold this towel on that ear. What! Give me that damn thing! He took the towel and held it to the side of his head to catch the blood. He started walking around in a daze then ended up outside in the front yard. Baby; where are you going; come here! Oh my God! Lisa picked up the phone and called the ambulance.

Scotty was incoherent and staggering from the tremendous amount of blood he was losing. Everyone on the block was now outside watching him as he wondered in to the street. His clothes were covered in blood as it continued to run down the side of his face. Police sirens in the distance became louder and louder as they got closer. Scotty fell down in the middle of the street just in front of his place.

The neighbors ran up to check on him. Hey Scott; hang in there man; help is on the way! Lisa stood outside on the porch crying and holding her head in disbelief as the neighbors gathered around her husband. Beep! Beep! The police car and ambulance blew their horns at the crowd as they approached.

Lisa stumbled down off the porch to go speak with the officers as they stepped on the scene. Ok people; I need everyone to move so the medics can help this gentleman. The paramedics kneeled down over Scott. Sir; can you hear me? Yes; yes. Alright; be still and let me take a look at your wound. You have a real nasty one here sir. I don't think we can save the ear. The other medic took a sanitized towel and cleaned the wound. Once he was done he packed it with gauze and wrapped his head with some more gauze.

You're going to be fine sir; we have to get you in the ambulance and take you to the hospital. Thank you sir! It's no problem buddy! Where's my wife! Lisa! Lisa! Yes honey; I'm here! She held him by the hand as they lifted him to the stretcher and rolled him on to the ambulance. Excuse me Ma'am! Yes officer! You're the wife; correct! Yes sir!

I'm Officer Rodgers! Hi officer; I'm Lisa! Nice to meet you Ma'am; can you tell me what happened here? Ah; we were arguing and I threw a knife at him. I didn't mean to hurt him. Ma'am; I smell alcohol; how much did you have to drink? Excuse me! I was asking; how much did you have to drink? Only a few glasses of wine sir! What's a few, Ma'am? Are we talking two or more like 4? I'm sorry officer; can I please go with my husband! Hold on ma'am; you need to answer the question! I don't remember sir! Now can I please go!

Lisa tried to walk away from the officer. Ma'am; please! I need for you to calm down and answer me. I already answered you! Ok; that's it! We're taking you down to the precinct ma'am! Why; what did I do! First off you're intoxicated and not complying with an officer. I answered your question! No; you did not! Secondly; we have to charge you with domestic violence and assault and battery. What the fuck! I need to be with my husband.

Ma'am; he's going to the hospital; you can speak with him after you go to court tomorrow. What; aint this a bitch! Come on ma'am let's go! The officer slapped the cuffs on Lisa and placed her in the back of the police car. Alright people; you can go about your business; there's nothing more to see here.

The officers got in their car, started it, turned off the sirens and followed the ambulance as they left the Long Island suburb. Bam! Bam! Bam! Ma'am; stop kicking the window! Bam! Bam! Bam! Lisa had her back on the seat and feet up in the air, kicking the back door window with all her strength.

Bam! Bam! Bam! Officer Rogers; stop the car! Rogers slowed down at his partner's request. Pull over here man. He parked the patrol car over by the curb. Bam! Bam! Bam! Ma'am; this is your last warning; stop kicking the window. The officers spoke to her kindly from the front seat.

Fuck you pig! Bam! Bam! Bam! The officer turned off the engine and they both exited the vehicle. Rogers opened the back door. Ma'am, get out of the car please! Fuck you!

Puh! Lisa spit at the officer. Buzz! Buzz! Ohhhh-Ohhhh-Ohhhh. Ma'am; just relax! Lisa fell back on the seat as the two wires from the taser stuck to her chest.

As she lay there motionless her body became still, eyes closed and all was now quiet. The officers closed the door and returned to the front seat. Damn boy; she was a live one! Yeah; she's more than a handful! Ha-ha! I sure hate it for her husband; I know he catches hell. You can say that again Rogers!

He starts the patrol car, turns on the sirens and they head to the precinct. Only in New York buddy; only in New York! The patrol car disappears in traffic in route to headquarters. Amidst the chaos, traffic continues as normal and the locals went about their day. Although tragic, Lisa's story was only one of many, in a city of millions.

Thank you for reading; Book 1 of Adoration; Love Unconditional. The first entry of Antwan 'Ant' Bank$ Erotic Love Series. In Book 2 of Adoration Jeron and Tim plan for their Grand Opening, Tonya and Simone enjoy the spoils of Love; in their own different ways.

Scott and Lisa come to a crossroad in their relationship. Craig and Sonya; enjoy success, love and happiness but Sonya soon finds out, that loving Craig comes with a price.

Please visit our site for updates on upcoming events and new releases from PrintHouse Books. (PrintHouseBooks.com)

If you enjoyed this Novel; be sure to check out other titles from ANTWAN 'ANT' BANK$. Available everywhere books are sold.

Isbn 978-0-615-59946-5

MADE is about Andy Cooper; a military vet, turned hustler, turned Gangster, turned Crime Boss. His marriage is on the rocks; fresh out of the military, AC finds himself broke and lost with a Wife and three kids to feed. Trapped in Sin City and working any job he can get from day to day, to make ends meet. Hating the state of mind he's in right now, a really fucked up way to be! Gone are the days when Uncle Sam paid for housing, day care and groceries.

Now, all own his own again, with no idea of where life is going to take him. One thing for sure, Andy "AC" Cooper no longer wanted to wear that Army uniform another day. Coop loved every minute of it and would not trade it for the world but the next chapter of his life was about to start. It just so happen that he landed in Las Vegas, one of the hardest cities to make it in, it is truly the land of the Hustler. What the outsiders don't know is that beneath the bright neon lights, the delicious buffets and luxurious casino's, lays a whole different world that would eventually suck him in.

Isbn- 978-0-9886428-2-9

In The Party Life, the collection of spirits; were some of my favorites to mix for the thousands of customer's that I served as a bartender back in my 20's. During 1995 - 1996, I worked as a bartender in several Las Vegas Clubs and had a damn good time doing it! I've included a few recipes I picked up from fellow bartenders, some from customers and most I've learned from bartending school.

Mixology is an art and if mastered one can make a really good living serving spirits and conversing with the people you serve at your bar. If you're a bartender looking for some new drinks or you're just someone interested in mixing up some new drinks in your kitchen. This book of spirits is for you. Welcome to the Party Life and remember to drink responsibly.

PRINTHOUSE BOOKS
PRESENTS

F.I.T.H.

What happens:
when bullying goes too far!

A must read for any Parent, Teacher or Kid

ANTWAN 'ANT' BANKS
A Coming of Age, Psychotic Drama

Isbn – 978-0-9886428-1-2

Earlier in the mid 80's and early 90's; I had the unfortunate opportunity of being friends or acquaintances with two special individuals. Now that I am thinking about it, maybe it wasn't unfortunate but faith that we crossed paths. Their stories we're similar, even though they happened at different times and in two separate parts of the world.

It is through my God given gift that I will deliver their message; through Eric; F.I.T.H's main character. I find it my destiny to help others see life as they did; at tragic moments in both their lives. The time and location of events and names have been changed to protect them and their victim's families. Hopefully this story will show why it's not cool to be a bully but deadly, when you factor in all the consequences.

PRINTHOUSEBOOKS.COM

Read it, Enjoy it, Tell a friend!